Sleeping Partners

In 1985, the beautiful and academically gifted Susannah Farrar, recently graduated with a first-class degree, makes a fateful decision – a decision that will be crucial to the future of both herself and her unborn child ...

Ten years later, while attending a craft weekend in Cloughton's Crossley Hall accompanied by her son Luke, she is shocked to see Adam Holroyd, a friend from her student days, playing in the 'band'. Why is she so keen to keep Luke away from him? And why is she so worried to hear that a stranger outside his school has been asking for him by name?

Towards the end of the evening a mysterious phone call takes Susannah away from the hall. Her son and her friend await her return ... and wait ... and wait.

In the early hours of the following morning, Chief Inspector Browne and Detective Constable Jennie Taylor of Cloughton CID are called upon to explain why a woman has been found huddled in a local bus shelter.

More importantly, they must track down who inflicted her fatal wounds ...

By the same author:

THE DEAD DO NOT PRAISE
FEAST INTO MOURNING
NO PLEASURE IN DEATH
THE WAY OF A SERPENT
DOWNHILL TO DEATH

Sleeping Partners

Pauline Bell

MACMILLAN

First published 1995 by Macmillan

an imprint of Macmillan General Books
25 Eccleston Place London SW1W 9NF
and Basingstoke

Associated companies throughout the world

ISBN 0 333 64766 1

9 8 7 6 5 4 3 2 1

A CIP catalogue record for this book is available from
the British Library

Phototypeset by Intype, London

Printed by Mackays of Chatham PLC, Chatham, Kent

In memory of
Mary Bell,
my mother-in-law

I am indebted to the early music group,
The Seeds of Time, of Halifax.

With my usual gratitude and thanks
to David and Lesley Lord

Prologue

When Vanessa Smith – driving past Crossley Hall towards the centre of Cloughton – saw the woman stumble and clutch a telegraph pole for support, her first reaction was to check the time by the dashboard clock. 'Not a minute after eleven,' her father had said, 'and don't bother thinking up any good excuses. If you're out in my car, that's the deadline.'

She knew he meant it and she was cutting it a bit fine already. Still, the woman looked in a bad way. She couldn't just drive on and leave her.

Vanessa drew up alongside the pole, shuffled across to the passenger seat and paused for several seconds to consider the situation. She was quite near one end of the town precinct but neither the windscreen nor the wing mirrors afforded sight of another living soul, just a double string of lights too widely spaced to be reassuring.

On her left, beyond the pavement and an eight-foot stone wall, lay the parkland belonging to Crossley Hall, of which she and her young man had recently availed themselves. Re-clad in his leathers, he – and his motorbike – would be halfway back to Huddersfield by now. There were houses to her right but their gardens, sloping steeply up the hillside, were long and the inhabitants were well out of earshot.

The woman, a mere foot and a half from the front passenger door, seemed oblivious to the proximity of the car. Immobile, she leaned her head against the wooden

1

pole, her eyes closed, the knuckles of her clutching hands white.

Vanessa flattened her nose against the window and debated with herself a few seconds more before the influence of five years of girl guiding finally made up her mind.

Resolute, now that the decision was made, she climbed out. She remembered to keep her voice calm, pitched low. 'Are you hurt? Tell me what happened.'

There was no response. The figure remained frozen to the pole. With a mixture of panic and revulsion, Vanessa registered that the woman's sleeve had a stain, dark and wet. She forced herself to touch the hand. The woman flinched and more of the dark wetness welled from the slit in the fabric of the sleeve. Vanessa was repelled but relieved. The woman was a victim, no longer a threat. With increasing confidence, she took the uninjured arm, prising it away from the pole. This time the woman moved with her, unresisting.

'The hospital's less than a mile away. Shall we get you there?' Steadying the woman with one hand, she eased herself back into the passenger seat and reached behind her for the travelling rug.

She apologized. 'Don't be offended, but my father will go mad if you bleed all over his precious upholstery. I can wash this.' She lowered the woman on to the rug, tucked her legs tidily in front of the seat and fastened the belt round her. Back in the driving seat, she resisted the impulse to ask further questions. The woman was obviously in shock. She should be left in peace until delivered to someone qualified to treat her.

Vanessa drove in silence, switching on the wipers as the first, rain-laden gusts of a threatened downpour obscured the windscreen. Less than five minutes saw her car entering the hospital grounds and she was relieved to see that the woman had opened her eyes. Though still subdued, she seemed to have snapped out of her trance and to understand as Vanessa indicated the now pouring rain.

2

'I'll stop outside the entrance to casualty and see you inside. I'll have to go and park the car then. I can't leave it here blocking the way. I'll have to make a phone call too, but after that I'll come and wait with you until some-one can sort you out.'

There was no sound but the lips moved, possibly mouthing thanks. Vanessa walked round the car, ready to support her passenger into the building, but the patient had rallied and headed for the swing doors under her own steam. Vanessa hesitated but a car drew up behind hers and blasted its horn. She climbed back into her father's Cavalier, drove the fifty-odd yards to the visitors' car park and lined up neatly behind a decrepit Fiesta.

Should she find a public telephone and ring home now? She'd better check on the woman first. Father would understand when he heard the full story. Strict he cer-tainly was, but not totally unreasonable. She pulled up the hood of her anorak and dashed across the hospital forecourt. The casualty department's waiting room was crowded but she noted approvingly that there was no sign of her protégée. Someone had obviously recognized her need for immediate attention.

Relieved of one anxiety, Vanessa thought she had better find a telephone and make peace with her father. Then she would make herself known at the casualty reception desk as the woman's temporary guardian. Provided that the doctors did not wish to admit her, she might as well complete her Good Samaritan act and save the woman an interminable wait for an ambulance by offering her a lift home.

1985

Part I

Chapter One

Heads turned as, with clanking and squeaking, the main hall doors were opened and bolted back. The students and the assorted visitors they had invited to witness their triumphs obeyed this signal to hush their chattering. The sun, which had been patterning the walls and floor through two areas of stained glass, suddenly disappeared. A mellow suggestion of tradition and antiquity disappeared with it and the hall was revealed for what it was, a wood-panelled box, a mere section of the huge concrete and glass cube that formed the university main building, a poor relation even of red brick.

Rows of tubular metal chairs with brown canvas seats married ill with graduate gowns, the rich colours of silk hoods and the general air of festivity and excitement. There was no dignity. It was Dr Jonathan Milton's opinion that institutions where the traditions had not developed over the years should have a style of their own to celebrate their annual successes.

This was a polytechnic, whatever the fancy name bestowed upon it by the Secretary of State. Its aping of Oxbridge customs and dress, without the architecture to match, produced an ambience half sleazy, half comic.

Dr Milton rose to his feet along with the rest of the massed throng as the Vice-Chancellor and his chosen acolytes processed down the long aisle to the platform. His resentment at not being of their company lessened slightly as he looked down on them. The ordinariness of their faces

7

was emphasized by their splendid robes and the anticlimax of their entry mocked by the badly recorded and feebly crackling music issuing from the speakers fixed to the walls. One of them needed discreet help to make it up the steps to the miniature thrones set out for them.

As he sank back into his rear-platform seat – his elders, apparently deemed his betters, being settled – Dr Milton sprawled comfortably and found it in him to sympathize with them. Less fit physically, though not, he assured himself, academically, they had to sit up straight in their prominent places and appear enthralled by the tedious ritual of yet another Presentation of Degrees.

It was the first such occasion, apart from his own graduation, for the young assistant lecturer beside him, who defended the students' euphoria and his own. 'Their hard work's being rewarded . . . their talent recognized . . . their sacrifices proved worthwhile.'

Milton thought it probable that the sacrifices had been more on the part of the assembled proud parents than their undergraduate offspring. In an undertone he continued the needling of his companion with which he had been relieving his boredom as they waited for the ceremony to begin. 'They're a fairly nondescript lot this time. The industrious ones have achieved as much as industry can achieve but there's hardly a ha'p'orth of real talent among the lot of them.'

The assistant lecturer was emboldened by indignation. 'Not the sort of talent you look for.' Realizing that he had been neither oblique nor witty, merely reckless, he hastily changed the subject. 'Someone told me the video camera broke down last year.'

Milton rearranged his lengthy cramped legs and answered the second remark. 'Yes, the proud mamas make it quite a little money-spinner. I'm glad to hear it whirring away this afternoon.'

The cameraman duly recorded opening addresses and an industriously played orchestral item before concentrat-

8

ing on the individual new graduates as they came to the platform to receive their degree certificates.

'Here come something worth recording for posterity.' Both dons watched the girl currently approaching the guest of honour, her half smile acknowledging the rise in volume and enthusiasm of the applause. Her dark skirt was of a length to hint at dimpled knees whilst the white blouse dipped at the neck as low as possible without revealing any cleavage. The heavy silk graduate gown was worn with a tacit promise to reveal all on a more suitable occasion.

Milton stuck his feet out into the side aisle and inclined his head in his junior's direction. 'One of the feast's tastier dishes – and the department's only first.'

'Susannah Farrar? Her little clique did seem to have most of the year's potential.'

Milton looked bored. 'Such as?'

'Matt Hanson?'

'His chief purpose in coming up was to pray for all his peers. He was more worried about missing a Bible study than an exam.' Milton shook his head to indicate incomprehension.

'Which is why he hasn't covered himself with glory – that and a weakness, surprising in combination with religious mania, for the sins of the flesh. Rumour had it he wasn't too heavenly minded to fall prey to Susannah's seductive charm.'

'Matt Hanson and Zannah? You're joking!'

The junior lecturer noted the careless diminutive but merely added, 'That young Indian chap, Urfan something, hung around with them too. He can't have been stupid to have got an upper second in his second language.'

'Singh? He's Pakistani.' Milton regarded balefully the line of students that snaked off into the dimness below the platform. 'Here come the also-rans.'

'I'm surprised Adam Holroyd's amongst them. What was it with him? Wine and women?'

9

'Song, actually. He's been a leading light of most of the college music societies. He set up an ancient music group and spent his grant on reproduction instruments instead of course books.'

'Maybe he should have read music.'

Milton rearranged his painful legs once again. 'I think not. It's a precarious career and bits of paper from academic institutions get you nowhere in it. English, even with a two-two, is a better bet.' His eyes raked the hall in an attempt to find Susannah. When he'd arrived, he had passed her on the terrace where she had been watching out for her family. She had studiously ignored him and he had continued on his way, via the glass-walled stairway to the main hall.

Pausing on the halfway landing to catch his breath, he had glanced down to the terrace and seen her greeting them, a stooped grey man, an anxious-looking blonde woman and another daughter. The sisters were alike, yet not alike. Both were fair, tallish, slim-waisted and long-legged. They probably shared the same bust measurement. The difference lay in how they bore it. He wondered whether the sister was older or younger. Older, probably. Hadn't Zannah mentioned a couple of children? The sister's shoulders were a mite rounded, causing an embryo replica of her father's stoop and a drooping of her full bosom. The blonde tresses were lank, probably several days towards their next washing. She hung back resentfully as the proud parents were reunited with their probably favoured daughter.

Suddenly, Milton located Susannah six rows back. She knew he was watching her.

Susannah Farrar stared straight ahead, avoiding his gaze. Today marked an end to Jonathan's pathetic puns on Paradise Lost and Paradise Regained and freedom from his pitiful fumblings. Mentally she reviewed the second-year students in the department, wondering which of them he would pick on to replace her – someone else who had come

10

up determined to try every experience university life had to offer, including the seduction of a don. She wished she had made a more challenging and satisfying choice.

Glancing back at the platform, she saw that the honoured guest, having disposed of the mountain of paper in front of him, sheet by rolled sheet, was about to address them. She listened for a couple of minutes before deciding that they had had better speakers at the prize-givings at her local comprehensive.

She'd listened avidly to them, hoping they'd tell her how to pull herself up by her bootstrings – and some of them had not disappointed her. She suspected that the claim of today's guest to harangue the assembly was a hefty bequest made to the college by his father and the hope that he would follow suit. She cut him out and tuned in to her own confused feelings as she reviewed the last three years.

She had come here to her own personal heaven, from grinding poverty to the riches of a local authority grant. In her first term it had shocked her that her fellow students found they could not live on it. She had left cultural sterility for a world of literature and music that she hoped would stretch her mind and unbind her imagination. Above all, she had come from the unwelcome proximity of two parents and a sister crammed into four rooms, to the bliss of privacy whenever she chose to shut her door. She had discovered the stepping stones to a good life. And now, with the river crossed, she'd blown it.

She had expected today's ceremony to be less than awe-inspiring but had hoped for dignity. It had turned out to be farcical, from the first barely recognizable strains that had crackled out of the speakers as the doors opened. 'Gaudeamus igitur!' Really! Perhaps the organizer of this inglorious event, as he mentally surveyed the serried ranks of geriatric academics in their pitiful fancy dress, had been motivated in his choice of music by a sense of humour as spiteful as her own.

She looked at the cream of academe, still enthroned on

11

the platform, propped up by their stiff silks, whilst the guest droned on, then returned to her own musings. Big hills seemed to grow smaller as you toiled up them. Three years ago a degree had been the be-all and end-all of her existence. Now she looked up and down the rows of students. If all these ordinary folk could graduate, something else was needed to separate off the high flyers.

Only, now she'd clipped her own wings and would be flying nowhere. And to compound her misery, she would soon be required to add ludicrous cap to the voluminous gown she was wearing and to simper for the photographer. Her parents would embarrass her with their awe, oblivious to the fact that she was only one of thousands, this year alone, who had attained this small success.

The speaker, thank goodness, was beginning his final, empty peroration. 'What you young men and women must remember is that it's not your circumstances but your attitude towards them that matters. What a potential failure sees as a disaster, an achiever views as an opportunity.'

Somehow the words penetrated. Susannah sat immobile, transfixed by the notion. Maybe she hadn't blown it after all. Maybe she would turn her disaster into an opportunity. The speaker was perfectly right, a genius in fact. Perhaps she could face the camera with equanimity, even enjoy the 'slap-up family meal in a restaurant' that her father had been saving up for to celebrate her graduation.

She was pleased to see the Vice-Chancellor and his train make their exit with their guest by a door at the back of the platform. The ludicrous processing was not to be repeated. Fighting her way through the crowd to the area where her parents and sister had been sitting, she claimed them, returned their hugs, then excused herself. 'Could you wait here for just a moment?' She would do it now, before her courage failed her. 'I need a quick word with my tutor.'

Matt Hanson's feet sank into the thick, moss-green carpet. Over his head, chandeliers held low-wattage bulbs that shed sufficient light to reflect on the crystal hangings but not enough to spoil the effect of the flickering candles set out on all the occupied tables below and held by answering many-faceted crystal stands. The flames were reflected too in the polished wooden tabletops, except where they were covered with crisp linen placemats.

There were flowers, even on the unoccupied tables, harmonizing with the colours of the room. No paper and silk in the little vases, but blooms delivered fresh each morning along with the greengroceries for the day's menus. Each tiny, individual arrangement, if he bent over it, would have its individual scent that mingled with that of the food, the wines and the cigar smoke.

Matt enjoyed luxury. It gave him active, positive pleasure. A long time ago he had thought that everyone felt the same but had soon realized this was not so. Grace, his twin sister, for instance, certainly did not and he suspected that his father valued his very comfortable and affluent life not so much for its own sake as because it marked him out as rich and successful, or 'blessed by the Lord's favour' as he preferred to call it. His mother called it nothing, but accepted it as her birthright, increased as her marriage portion and shared with her offspring, one of whom she considered did not deserve it and the other who mocked it. Matt made an art of enjoying the indulgence of his physical senses. Privately, in his head, he coined phrases to describe and encapsulate the sensations of pleasure that being rich made possible for him. It was one of his talents – maybe his only talent.

He wished his father could enjoy his easy life more honestly, could drop his Puritan pose and wear the true colours of the Epicurean he was. He felt certain that

13

underneath all the pious posing and posturing his father too was an unbeliever. He did not realize it, of course. It was himself he was so assiduously deceiving rather than the rest of the world.

As an obsequious waiter pulled back chairs for them, Matt asked himself if he could be sure that it had really been Susannah he had seen with that other, shabby, drooping girl, the little stooping man in the shiny suit and the dowdy woman. Surely they could not be her family. They had disappeared into Barry's Bistro. He could remember Susannah refusing to go there with Adam. Adam had been offended and after that they had seemed to lose interest in one another. Zannah would enjoy this place. His father's generous allowance had enabled him to wine and dine a couple of girls here but he had never brought her. She wouldn't quite have fitted in, although she was certainly a cut above Barry's.

The waiter was bringing the menus, huge and colourful. As they opened them each of his family disappeared from the other's view. His father ordered for two after much deliberation but no consultation with his mother. Matt smiled to himself as he remembered an enforced attendance at a 'weekly meeting' during his last vac. Perhaps 'forced' was unfair. He had been forced only by his desire to enjoy all the advantages of an approved and exemplary son. His father had addressed the mid-week attenders at length on the subject of the vegetarian diet that the prophet Daniel had insisted on inflicting upon himself and his three unfortunate friends.

He heard again the slight whistle of his father's breath escaping between his two widely spaced front teeth as he announced his text. ' "But Daniel purposed in his heart that he would not defile himself with the portion of the king's meat, nor with the wine that he drank . . ." '

' "Let them give us pulses to eat and water to drink." '

Matt suddenly realized that he had spoken aloud and saw that his father, too, had remembered his address. He shook his head, smiling benevolently and replied, as Matt had expected, with another text. ' "To everything there is a season and a time to every purpose under heaven . . ." '

His sister, sitting opposite, continued the passage in a neutral tone, ' " . . . every man should eat and drink and enjoy the good of all his labour, it is the gift of God." '

'Exactly.' Matt's father accepted the buttered asparagus that the waiter was deferentially offering.

Matt sighed. How could Grace remember such reams of the stuff when she cared about it even less than he did? He caught her wink as he received his avocado with its cargo of shellfish, floating in a sea of Marie Rose. Should he plead a pressing call of nature? It would serve no purpose. They would wait for him and everyone's food would spoil. Instead, he lowered his head and hid his face as his father rose to his feet. His grace was loud and fervent.

This was a first-class restaurant. Most of its well-bred clientele averted their eyes and went on with their own conversations. The rest sat silent, frozen, forcing themselves not to stare. Matt almost preferred it when they did. Eventually he looked up and began to eat.

Matt's mother, having swiftly dispatched her French onion soup, indicated that she was no more impressed with his lower second than his tutor had been. 'You never said there were so many kinds of degrees, but then you wouldn't, I suppose, if you were beaten by a girl.'

Grace took his part. 'It wasn't a competition, Mother.'

She dismissed her offspring with a toss of her head and turned to her husband. 'I think he spent too much time at all these meetings . . .'

Matt watched his father become even more the patriarch. 'If his fellow students neglected their share of the burden of spreading the Word then he had no choice. You wouldn't put academic glory before the saving of even one student's soul?' Matt saw that his three-year absence from home had not cured his parents' habit of

15

talking as though he were not there. He was no longer used to it and it irritated him. 'Personally, I'm glad he wasn't in the position of the girl with the only first. It would have been a great temptation to self-glorification. I'm only thankful that he had his priorities right.'

Why, Matt asked himself, had he spent his undergraduate time in so much religious activity? His father, of course, had expected him to join the college Christian Union and had enquired minutely into its activities – and they accepted no half measures. Besides, when he had first gone up, they had been the only sort of people he understood or knew how to treat. And it kept his father supplying the twice-termly cheques.

He had stopped listening to the conversation but tuned in again to catch yet another piece of Holy Writ. 'Oh well, all things work together for good . . .' His father rarely finished quoting a text, assuming his hearers were as deeply steeped in the Scriptures as he was. Matt had learned at eight years old that no one checked it was his Bible he was reading when his mother left his light on for the half hour after he had been put to bed. He therefore knew the beginning of all his father's favourite texts and the end of none. As his father was fairly well-versed in literature too, the three years of his English course had been useful to him in differentiating between chunks of Scripture, English proverbs and the plays of Shakespeare.

As the waiter served the main course, his parents continued to discuss him. 'And the Lord didn't fail him. He has his degree – though he could have done his bit for Hanson's without it.'

'No one at church,' Grace pointed out helpfully, 'knows one degree from another.' She knew this was her mother's chief concern.

George Hanson attacked his 32-ounce steak and regarded his son genially. 'I suppose, after two years of having a "long vac" you'll be wanting a bit of a holiday before launching into your working life.'

16

Matt shook his head. 'No, I want to buckle down straight away and become a working man.' He ignored Grace's mouthing of 'Creep' and basked in his father's approval.

'I'd better have "and Son" painted in tomorrow morning.'

Grace asked innocently, 'And when I've finished my course?'

'You can be a virtuous woman.' His father was perfectly serious. ' " . . . for her price is above rubies." '

Here were texts that Matthew did know. He had discovered whilst still at junior school what a mine of ammunition for baiting his twin was to be found in the third chapter of Ecclesiastes. ' "She seeketh wool and flax and worketh willingly with her hands." ' He watched gleefully as Grace scowled. ' "She riseth also whilst it is yet night and giveth meat to her household . . . With the fruit of her hands she planteth a vineyard." ' Grace had abandoned her chicken Kiev and was red with rage. ' "She is not afraid of the snow for her household: for all her household are clothed with scarlet." '

Matt was not sure at which point his father's beam of delight at this demonstration of his familiarity with the Old Testament became a frown at the realization that it was being mocked. 'That will do, Matthew. Grace, eat your dinner, dear. You mustn't waste good food.' Matt recognized the change of tone and desisted immediately. Now was not the time to annoy him. Nothing must go wrong with his plans to take his place in the family firm as soon as it could be arranged.

Grace had no wish to be employed by her father. At fifteen she had known that she wanted to be a doctor and had had the sense to tell their father that she wanted to be a nurse – a nice womanly profession for a girl preparing herself to be the helpmeet for a husband who would do the Lord's work whilst she brought up his children. She would be qualified in another two years and had plans to specialize in obstetrics. If her father wanted to call her a nurse, he was welcome.

He envied her, but there was no way he could win a similar peaceful independence for himself. The real reason for his lower second was that he wasn't very clever. He was lucky even to have got that, as Dr Milton had frequently told him. His father had been generous to his college and to that fact Matt owed the trouble they had taken over him. If he didn't go into the firm, what else could he do? The idea of one day having to control it terrified him.

Other things terrified him too.

His father had begun to talk about decorating the office he was to be given, about introducing him to his future colleagues. Matt wondered how soon he dare ask about his salary. He had intended to rent a small flat as soon as he had a job but now it might be wiser to stay under the paternal roof for a while. It was a good thing his parents expected him to tithe his income. He was going to have to be more generous than that. It was unlikely that one-tenth of his starting salary would be anything like the sum required. Was there any chance of coming clean with his father and getting him to help him straighten things out? But how could he explain it?

Urfan Singh had decided not to tell his wife, Shahnaz, about any of his amorous adventures during his three years at university. She understood a man's needs and would very likely not have blamed him for any of them, but she might have imagined more than had actually happened. There seemed little point in upsetting her and even less in upsetting her father before he had seen his son-in-law through college and safely installed him in his computer business.

He was always glad to leave his English girls behind and go back to her. English girls thought bare flesh was attractive and seductive. Personally, he found no garment so tantalizing as a sari, sinuously skimming the figure, but filmy, semi-transparent, subtly suggestive. Though Susannah was beautiful in an English way, beside Shahnaz she was brash and cheap.

It seemed that the traditional way to celebrate being presented with a degree here was to go out for a meal with the family members who had supported and encouraged your three years of study. Urfan's father-in-law had arranged a great gathering of his own family at a nearby restaurant run by his younger brother.

The dhals and curries would be the finest but Urfan could work up no enthusiasm for the party. This evening was somehow an anticlimax. The ceremony itself had been a disappointment and had dissipated his euphoria. He felt a sudden nostalgia for his Punjabi village with its thousand or so people, its surrounding plains growing grain, sugar cane and yellow-flowering mustard. There would be roses on the hedges separating the fields.

People had the wrong idea about Pakistani villages. As a small boy he had never been acquainted with the dirty wretched shacks surrounding the big cities. There were trees in the village squares and beside the houses, and canals brought them clear water and fish. His village streets were narrow so that the buildings filled them with shade in the hot weather. Some of the houses had outer walls of smooth red clay from the edge of the lake but his father's house was more modern, built with cement and brick. He had played on the flat roof, slept there in the hot season and looked up at the stars, big and bright.

He wondered how Shahnaz would take to it all, getting water from the hand pump outside, drawing down rich buffalo milk and turning it into butter and cheese, spraying everything, ineffectively, against the flies and mosquitoes. It wouldn't be easy. And it wasn't what Uma and Shain were used to. He couldn't quite see his wife sitting with the other women on a woven rug on the floor, making baskets and mats, embroidering saris. And she

19

would find the lack of privacy quite unacceptable. In his family, even defecation was a social occasion.

An extended trip back there was not really a practical proposition. He had better get ready and go to the feast with good grace and in all the regalia. In the Easter vac, when Shahnaz's father had called him sahajdhari, it had been only half in fun. He wasn't expected to keep his hair uncut in England, and now he didn't even have a beard, but tonight he would wear the kaccha and kara and carry his kirpan. He would have no trouble managing to appear teetotal. There would be no alcohol to tempt him.

He would take one more turn round the terrace with Shahnaz beside him to show his fellow students exactly how a beautiful lady should look and behave, and then he would put both his Punjabi village and his English university behind him.

Suddenly, Susannah came out through the french windows of the refectory and crossed the terrace towards them. She greeted Shahnaz politely, shook hands with his father-in-law and asked for a word with Urfan in private. 'We'll be very quick,' she assured his visitors. 'Just a last bit of university business.'

When he returned to Shahnaz, his brown face was as pale as it could be.

Jonathan Milton could equal, possibly outdo, his students in the field of sexual gymnastics but he was not a great drinker. His gin and tonic in the union bar today was a mark of real celebration. But what, he asked himself, was he celebrating, exactly?

Probably it was the prospect of spending the summer with his wife, he decided. Sheila knew of his little ways with the students. She had been one of them herself, though in those days his philandering had been a little more discreet, and the setting, if not his own position in it, more prestigious – Cambridge, in fact. He had left an assistant lecturer's-post there in the year that they married, the same year Sheila took her degree. Since then, he had progressed, through posts at Bristol and Reading, to his present chair.

He supposed, given the chance, he would have changed little of his past life.

Sheila had looked good today. He wondered how many more years of ripe womanhood remained for her before the bloom began to fade? He had paraded her in front of Joy Dennis, the little redhead he had his eye on for the Michaelmas term. He thought he had dropped enough gentle hints to ensure that he would find her sitting in his tutorial sessions. She was quite a different type from Susannah and not likely to cause him quite so much hassle. It looked as though this year's hassle was going to linger on after Susannah's departure.

He pondered the matter as he waited for his wife. Soon, Sheila emerged from the Ladies and he indicated the glass he had waiting for her. 'There won't be a restaurant in the whole town where we can count on not being accosted by proud parents and their embarrassed offspring. Let's eat at home.'

They did not have drinking habits in common. She handed over her glass, already empty. 'That one never touched the sides. If you want me to cook, I'll need softening up.'

Dutifully, he obtained a refill. 'Make it the last here, eh? I'll do the cooking.' He could hardly wait to be at home with her. It was a good marriage on the whole. They had both broken their conventional church vows but, over the years, each of them had stuck roughly to their tacit agreement. She was there, decorative and attentive, on academic occasions, so that dewy-fresh students entertained no hopes of their liaisons with him becoming permanent. He was there, on local government occasions, to help lard her speeches with amusing and apposite quotations, to ask the odd useful question from next to the back row and to initiate a bit of friendly heckling, much more use than any suspect, planted support.

They were both always busy, seemingly dependent on each other to a very small degree, yet each knowing the other could be relied upon utterly, should the occasion require it.

Earlier, Sheila had seen him in earnest conversation with Susannah and had effortlessly plucked him away. They had both enjoyed Susannah's surprised expression, half angry, half admiring, and he'd known the girl would study the technique and copy it. He'd thanked Sheila more sincerely than she realized for rescuing him. What Susannah had had to say had given him pause for thought.

'I have to be nice to them on their big day.'

She'd brushed aside his excuse. 'Such hypocrisy! You're the very opposite of Blake's Little Black Boy.' He'd raised his eyebrows enquiringly. ' "And you are white, but O! your soul is black." '

They'd giggled as, hand on heart, he protested, 'That's only the impression you get. Really, I'm like Gunga Din.

>An' for all 'is dirty 'ide,
>'E was white, clear white inside
>When 'e went to tend the wounded under fire.'

'That girl wasn't under fire. She'd demolished the enemy, then eaten them for supper. She was still licking her lips.'

'So long as she wasn't licking mine, you have nothing to complain about.'

They had walked across the car park and stopped by the BMW. She climbed into the passenger seat beside him and he regarded her fondly. This was his woman. Susannah was just a bird of passage and should remain so, at whatever cost. He'd take Sheila abroad this summer, somewhere exotic but unfashionable where no one would know them. He'd fix it tomorrow.

But Sheila had other ideas. As he reached with the key

towards the ignition, she pulled his hand away and on to her lap. 'Jon, you know I told you Crawshaw was having to give up his seat after his last heart attack? The by-election's scheduled for September. Don spoke to me this morning. They're offering me the candidature! I need to spend a bit of time over the summer getting familiar with his patch.'

Milton's spirits fell. He had not been counting on the Caribbean or the Far East – but did the retiring member have to represent a constituency in *Birmingham*? And he could see from her expression that there was more.

'Come on, out with it. What else?'

She shrugged. 'Nothing really – it's just – well, we're going to need to be squeaky-clean whilst everyone's getting used to me. I was wondering if you could fix up something a bit more low-key next term, with someone a bit less flamboyant.'

Milton swallowed hard. Joy would be just the job. He was even willing, in Sheila's best interests, to become a reformed character for next year. It was just that the repercussions of last year were not over yet.

1995

Part II

Chapter Two

Urfan Singh had been unimpressed by his first experience of an Anglican church wedding. The men had worn clothes that were undistinguishable from the ones they wore for funerals, and although the woman, an old school friend of his wife, had been pretty, she had looked washed out and colourless in bridal white. Even the elegant guests had, on the whole, adhered to the black and white theme and the revels afterwards had been very subdued.

He knew Shahnaz, like himself, had been comparing it with their own wedding, twelve years ago now. That had been a very different affair. Three hundred guests had come to celebrate with the family. His hands had trembled as he'd bound his turban and outlined his eyes with kohl. Shahnaz had been weighted down with heavy gold jewellery, necklaces, earrings and bangles. The stage holding the Holy Book had been covered in fine scarves that his mother had embroidered with stars. There had been flowers everywhere and coins on the stage had glittered, offerings for the temple from their guests.

His father-in-law had brought Shahnaz to him in her red salvar komise and led her to the stage to sit before the holy table. He felt again, now, the strangeness and excitement of having her there. He pitied this afternoon's bridegroom. He probably had no experience left to share with his bride that they had not already enjoyed. With Shahnaz, he had had everything still before him. He had hardly even conversed with her beyond stiff, formal phrases.

27

His English friends, now, thought it had been a great risk but their track record in marriage did not compare favourably with that of his own culture. He and Shahnaz had had similar religious traditions, codes of living, social values and customs. English girls got a poor deal, he thought, some of them anyway. The pretty ones and the outgoing ones were soon spoken for, but what of the plain-faced, good women who would be excellent mothers, efficient household managers and loyal, loving partners?

Of course, he had been delighted that Shahnaz combined these qualities with beauty – and she had passed on her comeliness to her daughters. He had been proud to sit beside her before the stage and tie his sash to her veil. They had circled the table together in a bubble of joy, oblivious of anything but each other. The priest had said his prayers and the ritual semolina had been offered to them and their guests. She had become his wife, his ticket to Britain, his chance of an education at an English university.

He'd made good. Even his father-in-law maintained that the capital invested in him had not been wasted. He had proved he was clever, had worked hard to provide for Shahnaz and his family according to the best Sikh traditions. Their eldest daughter, Uma, was presently studying upstairs. He could see through the window that the other two girls were gathering flowers under their mother's supervision.

Their last-born, eight days old and lying in a carrycot in the corner of the living room, began to cry. Urfan opened the window so that Shahnaz would hear. The cries intensified. Urfan watched as Shahnaz gave careful instructions to Shain and Manju before hurrying indoors. Quickly, she pacified the child by whatever mysterious means had been given to women and, mercifully, denied to men. Then she picked it up and crossed the room to offer it to him.

He hesitated, looking down at it as it peacefully slept again, then took it from her. He was not yet reconciled to the arrival of yet another daughter, but Shahnaz, in all respects a good Sikh wife, had been educated in an English grammar school. She'd told him that the English king, Henry the Eighth, could have saved himself a great deal of domestic disruption if he'd known that the sex of children is determined in the father's sperm.

He accepted the warm bundle from her and smiled at her over it. 'Perhaps we'll have a son next time.'

She was not smiling. 'We have another beautiful daughter this time.'

But he was capable of fathering a son. He had proved it and paid for it.

Adam Holroyd slipped the disc into his CD player and turned up the bass before switching on. The opening drum roll caused him the usual stirring of excitement. He turned the sound down a little rather than close the window on this unseasonably warm evening, then stood motionless, paying respect to the unbelievable soprano, pure, clear, yet powerful and confident. When the lower voices joined it, the music still pleased him but the first magic was gone for him.

He hoped that at least a few of his players would arrive before the piece finished. It would set the tone and standard for the evening's practice. He closed his eyes and concentrated fully. The sound was primitive, yet at the same time sophisticated. Maybe it was his own response that was primitive – or perhaps the melody appealed to what was primitive in his own nature.

Italian was supposed to be the most lyrical language but these Spanish phrases were equally athletically leaping and falling with the melody. Some of the excitement came from the omnipresent basic beat of the percussion that ran beneath whatever elaborate gymnastics were performed by the voices and instruments above it. Just occasionally the Clifton Consort played a few phrases to this standard, catching the enthusiasm of long-dead composers. Adam remembered the television series by that acme of early music specialists, David Munrow, which had entranced him in his infancy and led to his own small achievements with medieval and Renaissance instruments and to the formation of the Clifton Consort.

He glanced round the room that awaited its members, on the first floor at the front of his Georgian terrace near the centre of Bath. Haphazard was a flattering description of its furnishings. Colour-washed plaster and thin matting enhanced the acoustics. A venerable upright Bechstein backed on to one wall, with an electronic keyboard reared up against it. Cupboards full of music lined up opposite, one with hi-fi components stacked on top and another holding racks of tapes and discs.

A small table held his stand of wind instruments, the tallest reaching beyond the picture moulding. The tall cupboard behind the door contained the group's larger instruments. The doors stood open so that the viols and the hurdy-gurdy could be lifted out as their respective players arrived. On the large table in the alcove were glasses and several uncorked bottles, their murky contents already warming.

In the subdued light of two lamps it all appeared cosy, but the harsh central lights, necessary for reading their music when the practice began, would reveal a sort of shabby schoolroom. A circle of metal-strip folding music-stands matched one another, but the chairs in front of them were a motley collection, tubular-frame and canvas from a defunct church hall, two kitchen stools and several ladder-back dining chairs inherited from his parents.

Skirting a pile of assorted drums with a crowning tambourine, he went to the window and opened it wider. Once the practice began he knew he would be risking strange looks from passers-by and possibly complaints from his neighbours but the room was already warm and ten players, energetically blowing and bowing, would soon become uncomfortable. A car drew up at the gate and the first arrival made his way up the path.

Robert was smart in suit, white shirt and tie, hot-foot from his churchwarden's duties at Evensong. Adam's own perfunctory Sunday observance was at the local, high-Anglican early Eucharist where the minister gabbled his way through the service and communicated his congregation of seven in twenty-five minutes. Adam's attendance was the fulfilment of his duty, not so much to God as to rigorous grand-maternal instruction and example. Since his return he had dressed in comfortable cords and T-shirt. He remained in the window, knowing that Robert and the rest of the group would let themselves in at the unlocked kitchen door and make their own way upstairs. The two dogs could safely be left to deal with anyone who might avail himself of the privilege uninvited.

Another figure appeared at the gate, track-suited and breathless. Adam frowned. Simon was welcome to make the journey part of his weekly jogging stint but he wished he would arrive in time to take a quick shower before their musical activities began. The frown became a glower as he realized that Simon was accompanied. The girl for whom he opened the gate with a flourish wore high-heeled shoes and a summer dress that was really a sunsuit – a bit over the top for mid-October even if it was unusually warm. She was attractive though. Moving closer to the pane he peered up the road and saw Simon's car behind Robert's. So Simon had run only yards. Perhaps the girl was responsible for the breathlessness.

Adam was not pleased to see her. According to Simon this new recruit was an able musician. He was confident that if Simon had said it, it would be so, but there was no place for her at this rehearsal, the last before their programme at Crossley Hall on Saturday. It would waste precious time to explain things to her as they went along but it would be discourteous not to. He mustn't put her off. They'd need her when Sandra left them after this last gig. Simon had brought her along to their concert in Cambridge last month and now he couldn't remember her name. He was glad Robert had remained in the kitchen making a fuss of the dogs. They took more notice of him than of Simon and a bitten leg would not encourage the girl to rehearse here again. He was relieved to hear their feet on the stairs, accompanied by frenzied barking, and he crossed the room to set the disc to its beginning again and to fill the glasses.

He handed them out as the players came in, stopping in front of the girl with a friendly grin. 'Hello again. The first thing you need to know is that we run on red wine.' She accepted her glass and then moved across to the music centre looking for the empty CD case. Realizing it was in his pocket, Adam handed it over. 'It's the Hesperion XX, doing items from the Medinaceli Songbook.' He smiled at her. Maybe the sunsuit wasn't over the top if you had firm brown limbs and smooth slim shoulders.

She was unfamiliar with both the group and its music. 'Are they Spanish?'

Adam nodded. 'The songs are from the Kingdom of Castille around Philip II's time. The date 1597 is written on the first sheets of the original manuscript.' He saw to his relief that she was wearing one of those necklaces that had a name in fused metal letters slung on a fine chain. He thought them more suitable for young schoolgirls than for women in their early twenties but was grateful for this one. 'Do you speak Spanish, Karen?'

She shook her head. 'Not yet, but I've just started an evening class.'

They both stood for a moment, paying their respects to the castrato-soprano, before Adam broke the spell.

> 'Llora toda la corte
> cada qual quien mas podia –

32

' "All the court is mourning and each one cries as much as he can." ' He grinned. 'None of your twentieth-century British male stiff-upper-lip as Don Manrique's remains were honoured and escorted to his grave. Are you a soprano?'

She nodded. 'But not in his league.'

He surveyed her, leaving someone else to continue the conversation. She was in a league of her own. She had a curtain of honey-blonde hair like Susannah's. Maybe fair hair turned him or. What a question to be considering at thirty-two years of age. He didn't know what appealed to him in a woman. How could his own sexuality be so undeveloped, so unanalysed – especially when he had a son to prove he had a sexuality to examine?

Simon joined them and Adam poured wine for the rest of the company, now seated in their accustomed places on the assorted chairs. Simon distributed it as Adam took charge of the evening's business. 'Right, we'll loosen our fingers on something we like and know well – and something we're not playing on Saturday so we can just enjoy it. What about "The Punk's Delight"?' He realized the apparent spontaneity of the suggestion was rather spoiled by his having the ten relevant sheets of music in his hand but the piece was a popular one.

Robert smoothed a bent corner on his manuscript before arranging it on his stand and surveying the instrument at his feet. 'Shall we do it on recorders first and get your neighbours used to us being in action again before we use anything louder?' Recorders of various sizes were passed over heads. After accepting his bass, Robert fished under his chair for the sling, attached it to the little hook and slung the recorder from his neck, the cord disappearing into the folds of fat there.

Simon, recorderless, took up a tabor and gently drummed variations on the basic common time. With no music to follow he watched Karen, saw that she was familiar with the melody, and handed her the drum. Taking it, she

33

continued with the basic rhythm for half a dozen bars. Then, with a spark of mischief in her eyes, she began a frenzy of rhythmical adventures against the background of the recorder tune and harmonies. Adam was delighted. In the music the group played, rhythm was almost everything and the new girl's timing was immaculate. He felt an even greater satisfaction when she sheepishly laid down the drum at the end of the piece. 'That was a bit naughty,' she said. 'Such a simple tune needs a much less elaborate underpinning.' So, she was musically sensitive too.

Her gaze was direct, he observed. At least he could make some negative definitions concerning his ideal woman. She was not coy. Susannah had looked straight at him but in her case it was because she had displayed her wares. She watched to check that her interlocutor did not undervalue them.

Now that they had played themselves into a good mood Adam stopped to give them some details of their Saturday performance. 'Weather permitting we'll be outside in the afternoon. We'll have nothing abstruse, we'll just concentrate on the loud and the lively. We'll use Playford but there's no set programme. We'll see what they like and keep playing that. We want to attract people, not educate them.'

'What's the hall like?' one of the girls asked.

'Beautiful. It's timber-framed, begun mid-fifteenth century with additions up to the early seventeenth so it nicely spans the period of our programme. It used to have a minstrels' gallery but that's walled off now so the evening concert will be on a makeshift platform in the body of the Great Hall.'

'Good acoustics?'

'Excellent, though that'll be spoiled when the hall is packed with people. I hope the warm weather keeps up – it suits the instruments.'

'Are we doing the Bawdy Songs?'

Adam considered. 'We won't sing them in the after-

34

noon. There'll probably be a lot of children about. In the evening we'll have them in the second half when the punters have had a few interval drinks.'

They began to play again. Adam picked up the trombone with the narrow bell which, for the moment, had to substitute for a sackbut, and gave himself up to the joy of fitting his own part into the intricate pattern of a catch by Piero. Both Robert and Simon were in good voice tonight. He hoped their inevitable roaring at Bath City's Friday-night fixture in the Vauxhall Conference League wouldn't do too much damage.

He began to study the other musicians as they played. All of them wagged or tapped their toes to mark the basic rhythm, whatever their fingers were doing. Paul swayed gently from side to side, putting his right eye in peril from Laura's left elbow, which rose then fell on the first and second beats of the bar. Adam wondered what unconscious mannerisms marked his own playing and whether an audience would find them irritating, or, worse, amusing. Robert's face, wet with perspiration, was quite expressionless though his playing was sensitive and accurate. They stopped, and there was silence after the first successful run-through as they got over their amazement.

'Aren't the suspensions wonderful? We'll pause while you dry your tears and deal with the shivers up your spine.'

They grinned at him.

'Nothing serious went wrong did it?' asked Robert. 'When we began the first repeat Laura looked startled, as though it couldn't be right.'

'Don't worry, Robert, unless you see the same expression on the faces in the audience. Right, we'd better get on.'

Some instruments were exchanged and more were passed from the cupboard. Karen looked surprised. 'How many do each of you play?'

Simon shrugged. 'The aim is for us to play all the ones we've got – or most, anyway. We've all got jobs and families, for which we're thankful of course, but they keep us from getting to every rehearsal – or even every gig. We've a better chance of sticking to the programme we've promised if we're all as versatile as possible.'

Adam started them off again. Since they had played the difficult piece to concert standard, he was not surprised when some of the easier passages went sadly awry. 'You're playing this as though you'd never seen it before! This is the piece we're playing on Saturday, you know.' In the resentful silence he wondered if the original error might have been his own. His tone became more conciliatory. 'It doesn't help that no tempo is indicated. Once we're ten bars into it Gwynneth and Barry are slowing it down slightly and possibly I'm speeding it up. The difference is the root of all the trouble.'

Their next attempt was his reward for failing to conceal his impatience, feeble, hesitant, the rhythm correct but so deliberate that the melody became irrelevant. He let them finish. 'Well, I asked for that.'

'I count better when I'm on my second glass,' Robert remarked mournfully. Adam silently thanked him as a ripple of laughter went round and glasses were offered for refilling. From here it would be a downhill run, just the Playford Dances and the infamous Bawdy Songs. He wondered how Karen would react to them. 'I've seen an arrangement of the first one set a tone lower than ours. The bottom E really emphasizes the animal humour.'

Robert guffawed. 'You can't lower the tone of "The Old Fumbler" or "My Man John", surely?' The others grinned. 'Besides, I'm not as sure of my bottom E as I used to be.'

A raucous rendering of the selection of songs necessitated another round of drinks which made further serious rehearsal useless. They were looking forward to the Playford Dances, though, and Adam decided they would be a pleasant way to end the evening. He handed out the books. 'Let's do "Black Nag".'

For the hundredth time he wished the group was professional and could work under proper conditions. The shabby room and unmatching chairs mattered little and all his own spare cash was contributed towards instruments and other necessary gear. It was their time he wanted to buy, to improve the standard of their playing and to go after the contacts they needed in order to become better known. But he had a son to support and would have for some years yet. There was no getting away from his forty-hour stint in the library every week or his monthly cheque to the bank in Cloughton in Yorkshire. Susannah would make sure of that.

He wondered at Adam, the student, who had succumbed so quickly to her purely physical charms, in full knowledge of the self-orientated nature they gave substance to. An impressionable youth with tastes and opinions largely unformed, he had been no more highly sexed then than he was now, certainly he had not been promiscuous. Susannah's ample breasts and undeniably beautiful face had not occupied his thoughts overmuch. It was her vitality that had seduced him and her exciting animal greed for all the experiences she could wrench from life.

It had surprised him that he had figured on the list of men she adjudged suitable escorts and even that she had chosen to give birth to her child and take care of him. Adam had paid the dues demanded gladly, thankful to be released so easily from a relationship that had soon become irksome to both of them.

He reviewed his almost-celibate life since then. How likely was it, he wondered, that his substitution of musical for sexual pleasure was because he felt obliged to reveal to all future partners this brief relationship with his fellow undergraduate and its result. He could hardly pay serious court to another woman without revealing to her his corruptibility and its consequent drain on his future income. And, at what point should it be revealed?

37

This question had always cost him more agonizing than the facts themselves. It seemed presumptuous to explain all on a first outing, in anticipation of the girl's falling in love with him and wanting to share her life with him. And yet, he always felt uncomfortably deceitful if a second meeting was arranged with the girl still in ignorance. Maybe he took life and himself too seriously but he didn't think he could change that. It was simpler to manage his personal affairs without a woman. Would that he had realized this ten years before.

It suddenly struck Adam that he had always thought in terms of *Susannah's* child. And for the first time he felt an urge to meet his son. Its strength surprised him – and its belatedness. He had been a father for nine years and for that length of time had understood his situation only in terms of X pounds per month.

Surrounded by proud friends and relations, he had been preparing to go home after his degree presentation when Susannah had revealed her condition to him. In shock, he had been delighted to comply with her demand that he say nothing to his family and wait for her letter. It had contained a demand that he stay out of her life, apart from the standing order to his bank. It had given him her bank's Cloughton address but not her own.

A few months later, another letter had followed, with the same postmark but still no address, written, perhaps, in the first proud flush of motherhood, the next of life's experiences in which she intended to indulge herself. It informed him that her son, Luke Sebastian, would bear her own surname and that his birth certificate would not name his father. Nine years later, for the first time, he was angry. Why had it taken a decade for him to feel these paternal stirrings?

Never mind. He would stay on in Cloughton on Saturday night. He still paid his monthly allowance to her bank there, so presumably he could find out where Susannah was living and arrange to meet the child. It was his right.

It occurred to him that she might actually come to Crossley Hall. Since his order was still paid to the same branch of her bank, it was unlikely that she had moved away. She was not musical but this arts weekend seemed to have plenty to attract a culture-hungry woman and an intelligent boy.

Simon addressed him and, abruptly, he returned to his immediate surroundings. 'What do you want percussion on?'

'Whatever you fancy.'

Simon took the tambourine from the top of a pile of drums and they played through the next simple dance tune.

'Right, now twice as fast.'

They responded magnificently. Adam noticed that Karen, flushed and animated, was more than holding her own on one of the bass recorders.

'That last section was splendid,' he said when they'd finished. 'You were relaxed and fluent, and when you did make a mistake it didn't throw you. Play like that on Saturday.'

It was arranged that Karen would travel with them in the minibus and be part of the audience at the hall. Adam tried to decide how soon he should confess to her that he had a son.

Chapter Three

At a crossroads in one of the more salubrious suburbs of Birmingham stands the Grapes of Wrath. It is a quiet and efficient small hotel, much frequented and much approved by the better class of travelling businessman. It advertises itself only by word of mouth and a discreet, though hardly artistic, hanging sign that features a clenched fist and some unlikely-looking, bright blue berries, presumably grapes.

Its head barman was newly appointed; he was nearing the end of his first stint of duty in fact. He had been quite happy when the manager had explained to him that the bar had no official time to close and he would go off duty when he had cleared up after the last resident. He looked at his watch now and grimaced at his assistant. 'You might as well go, Chris. There's hardly likely to be a rush between now and morning.'

They both glared at the two remaining drinkers. Chris was tempted but then shook his head. 'I'd better stay, Bill. The state that pair are in, you might well need help.'

Bill was thankful. He pulled a pint for each of them, dropped the money ostentatiously into the till and pushed Chris's glass towards him. 'They didn't seem all that pleased to see each other when the older chap first came in. They got friendlier as they got drunker.'

'The one with the bald patch hasn't had more than three pints in halves but he's as pissed as his mate.' Chris downed half the contents of his glass in a gulp and peered morosely at the rest of the murky liquid.

Bill removed froth from his top lip with the back of his hand and glared at the rear view of their older customer. From his loud and slurred conversation, he had gathered that the man was a university teacher, who was on a 'sabbatical', whatever that might be. The younger man, whose tones were equally loud but much clearer, was one of the delegates at the conference that had taken over the whole of the top floor. He looked the part in smart dark suit, white shirt and sober tie. The professor bloke was a ragamuffin. It appeared that his name was Milton. Wasn't there a poet of that name? Very suitable.

He turned to Chris. 'Ever heard of Milton?'

Chris scratched his head. 'Milton Keynes, you mean? It's one of them new towns, in Northamptonshire, or it might be Bucks.' He nodded towards the drinkers. 'Do we have to stay here if they pass out?'

Bill gave up. If Chris hadn't heard of Milton, he would hardly know what a sabbatical was. He lifted the flap of the bar and walked over to his two customers. 'Will you be wanting anything more tonight?'

He tried to indicate, by the tone of his question, that he was expecting a refusal. In his brain, there was a flicker of a memory of an O-level Latin lesson. Didn't you stick *num* at the beginning of a sentence if you wanted a negative reply? Or was it *nonne*? He couldn't remember and regretted afresh that extra year at school that had gained him five useless O-levels, a dim memory of Latin adverbs and a vague impression of an intimidating poet called Milton. It had deprived him of the extra twelve months' dole money that most of his former classmates had collected.

He obviously had not got the intonation of the current question right. The businessman asked for two neat whiskies. There are nothing else to put away but Chris knelt behind the bar and suggestively slammed the cupboard

41

doors. When this signal was ignored, he wandered between the tables and switched off the television set.

He came back to the head barman, shaking his head. 'I don't understand it. They've both been in here several times before and made a couple of drinks last all night. They weren't together then though. They must have set one another off tonight.'

The burden of their complaints seemed to be the misdeeds of a girl they both knew, possibly called Anna. Wasn't it always a woman? The head barman wondered how old this one must be if she'd played dirty with both of them. The business chappie was youngish, no more than thirty or so, but the prof type was in his mid-fifties if he was a day – and well worn at that.

Chris contemplated turning off the fire. The central heating had been off now for more than an hour. He decided not to. The manager got very shirty about customer complaints and it was Bill's first night. Better not make any bother for him.

It was a great relief to them both when the older of the two customers finally slid slowly to the floor. Now Bill could take charge in the guise of being helpful. 'Not to worry, sir. He's no heavyweight. The three of us can manage him easily.'

They manoeuvred the comatose professor out of the bar, then Bill propped him against the wall whilst he turned and smartly locked the door behind him. He did not intend, after they had manhandled the casualty in and out of the lift and safely into his bed, to come down and find that his businessman friend had returned for a nightcap.

Chapter Four

Susannah Farrar had resigned herself to half an hour's wait whilst her son did his round of the swings and roundabouts in Crossley Hall's children's playground. However, seeing that the children currently playing on them were younger than himself, Luke affected to despise them and volunteered to show his mother the knot garden. He'd been given a talk about it when he'd visited the hall with his school the previous Wednesday, and now considered himself quite an expert. He prattled on happily as they made their way through the gloomy Yew Tunnel that led to it.

'It isn't the same knot garden that was planted when the house was built. They take a lot of looking after so they went out of fashion but they've copied this one out of a book.'

Susannah, primed by a quick scan of the official guide to the hall, was not to be outdone. 'This is an open knot design. That means gravel is used in the spaces between the hedges.' Her son was impressed.

'They're not privet like ours though, they're box hedges. Do you think they were cut tiny for little Tudor children?' Luke licked up the remains of his ice lolly, looked round for a litter bin, failed to find one and tucked the stained pink stick tidily into his pocket. 'Little Tudor children had different games from us, like archery and backgammon and hawking. What's hawking?'

Susannah shrugged. 'I'm not sure, but they played

skittles too. That's like the ten-pin bowling you sometimes do with Uncle Kevin.' They were both distracted from their competitive display of knowledge by the strains of a lively country dance tune. 'Sounds as though your band has started up. Shall we go and listen?'

Luke was already heading towards the sound. 'It's not a band. They're Elizabethan travelling players. Come on, it's in the orchard.'

Before re-entering the Yew Tunnel they took a last look at the south view of the house. The matt black and sparkling white of the decorative barge boards reminded Luke of another aspect of his school visit.

'We had to count how many different geometric patterns we could see in the walls of the house. Javed found three more than me but I found some Roman numbers carved on the beams. Mr Sandford said they were to show where the beams should be joined.' Mentioning his friend had set off another train of thought. 'Is Luke Farrar a Pakistani name as well as an English one?'

Susannah was startled. 'Why do you ask?'

'Oh, nothing.' The child skipped ahead and looked indignant at the angry tone of her command for him to come back.

'I asked you a question!'

He scampered back, anxious to be in her good books again. 'At hometime on Tuesday there was an Asian gentleman outside the school. He asked Javed if his name was Luke Farrar.'

'What did Javed say?'

She watched the child try to work out which version of the incident would dissipate her unaccountable displeasure.

'I'm not sure. I wasn't there. He told the man I was at my recorder club.' He hurried on, anticipating her next question. 'I didn't see him when I came out.'

Susannah, who had been parked outside school for several minutes that evening waiting for her son, anxiously tried to recapture the scene. She shook her head to clear it. 'Have you seen him since?'

The music called him but he was afraid to show his impatience. 'No.'

He was eyeing her warily and she pulled herself together, concealing her panic. 'Let's go and hear the music then.'

They made their way towards the 'orchard' with its remaining four trees, their branches heavy with red apples, and joined the thin gathering of listeners on the adjoining grassy slope. Once she was sure Luke's attention was firmly fixed on the Clifton Consort she began to assess the unexpected problem with which he had just presented her. Could the stranger outside the school have been Urfan? Had Luke got the story right? Maybe one of Javed's numerous Pakistani relatives had merely asked him where his friend Luke Farrar was, as they would normally be together as they came out of school. She knew she was clutching at straws. Luke could be trusted to relate an incident accurately and, judging from his little brown intelligent face, so could Javed. There was nothing she could do for the present, whatever the case. She looked around her, deliberately taking note of her surroundings and letting them distract her. The early music group had arranged themselves in the far corner of the orchard. She had seen one of the group, dressed in concert dress, in the ladies' loo at lunchtime and wondered how she would cope with her voluminous skirt. Only then had she realized the nature of the concert music, having been expecting some kind of military brass band. The medieval player had looked slightly ridiculous, queueing up with jean-clad girls and women in summer blouses but the whole group in costume made an attractive picture.

The girls had obviously followed their fancies amongst the fashions of the long period their music spanned. There was a white Puritan collar, several laced bodices and one dress had a long ruched panel set down each sleeve. All the female costumes were low cut at the front and long skirted. Some instruments were scattered on the grass under the shelter of a large golfing umbrella. There was opposition to the tunes they played from noisy birds, which only added to the period atmosphere. Unfortunately it was spoiled by their sitting on plastic chairs and by the fact that several of the group wore modern, plastic-rimmed spectacles.

The ducks on the river and the cows on the grass beyond it looked more interested in the entertainment than the human audience did, some of whose ears were plugged with attachments from their pocket radios, keeping them informed of the fortunes of their favoured football teams. A passer-by, attracted by a particularly loud and rhythmical offering, stared at the group in its antique attire before taking out his camera and snapping two exposures. Having done due obeisance to the arts, he joined the ice-cream queue. 'Snugbury's Dairy Ice Cream Sold Here' announced a garish banner. Snugbury was making a fortune. Susannah stepped quickly aside to protect her linen dress from a pop-eyed, open-mouthed infant who was offering the contents of his cone to all within reach of his flailing arms. Yet another dance began. Luke turned to her, grinning delightedly. 'I know this one.' To Susannah the pieces were indistinguishable. Luke wriggled closer. 'I wish I'd lived in the seventeenth century with lovely houses and music.'

'You wouldn't have liked what went with it,' she told him repressively. 'Look, they're going to sing.'

The musicians had laid down their instruments, arranged themselves standing in a half-circle and begun to sing what Susannah thought was a madrigal. Their voices were simultaneously sweet and strident and Susannah was reminded of the group of Salvation Army bandsmen who'd sung in the street every Christmas morning throughout her childhood. As the song proceeded Luke had gradually edged nearer and nearer to the performers.

She had kept beside him so that now they were at the front of the meagre audience. As the consort resumed their seats and took up their instruments again she looked hard at the player on the far left. When he turned to meet her gaze she received the second shock of the afternoon.

Adam had been aware of Susannah's presence from the moment she walked into the orchard. He realized as he caught sight of her that he had been looking out for her ever since their early arrival in the minibus.

It was ridiculously hot for October. Usually they unloaded and set up systematically and efficiently, each of them always having the same personal responsibilities. Today a couple of dazed and irritable wasps had caused mayhem amongst the women. Instruments and other belongings were dropped as some of them dodged hysterically to escape the angry buzzing.

Adam had felt physically weary before the group had even begun to play. They had left Bath at half past six this morning and he had done two stints of the five hours' driving. Usually he relaxed when the music began, however far they had travelled to perform it. This afternoon he had remained irritable and on edge without knowing why. He didn't want to renew his acquaintance with Susannah, but seeing her in the audience, he found he could at least relax, no longer wondering whether she would turn up.

As he played his eyes were fixed on the boy beside her. He was tallish for nine, slight rather than sturdy though by no means frail. Other children ran about and chased balls behind him but he stood for the most part grave and quiet, sometimes rapt. Susannah hadn't cowed him though. When he turned to speak to her his manner was eager. His hair was fair like his mother's, his features at this distance indistinguishable. How could he tempt him nearer?

The group finished its second rendering of 'Black Nag'.

'Shall we take a break?' Adam suggested. 'Let them come and handle the instruments whilst you give your lips a rest?'

Sandra foiled this ruse with a shake of her head. 'Quick, begin again before this tiny group disperses.'

He laid further plans. 'All right, "All in a garden green".' They performed it with no difficulty. 'Right, now twice the speed.' They responded magnificently. 'Again.'

Robert groaned. 'No jolly fear. We'll have that break you promised.'

Satisfied, Adam handed Karen a crumhorn. 'Take it to the kid at the front and invite everyone to come over and inspect the rest of the stuff.' She set off obediently, and Adam took his eyes off his son sufficiently long to appreciate the lithe figure and the gleaming fair outline of her head. The players relaxed as she demonstrated how the crumhorn worked and a good number of people clustered round her.

'Good idea of yours, Adam. That'll solve the problem of losing the audience while we warm up, tune the next set of instruments and secure the new music.' Robert proceeded to perform these chores, wincing as his fingers came into contact with the bare metal of his music stand which the sun had rendered too hot to touch. 'This is ridiculous in October. The back of my neck's burnt too.'

Simon stretched inelegantly. 'That's not the only disadvantage of playing outside. The wind's carrying some of the sound away from the people sitting in the shelter of the wall.'

'And my favourite phrase in "Black Nag" was completely lost in the roar of an aeroplane.'

'The publicity is substantially inaccurate. Did you read the poster about us on the gate? It's got "Medieval Minstrels" in huge letters. Only two items in either of our programmes are actually medieval.'

Adam ceased to listen to the musicians' chatter as a wave of frustrated anger swept over him. Karen was beckoning her listeners to follow her back to the performers' corner. Luke had made two eager strides after her when Susannah took his arm and pulled him back. After an ostentatious consultation of her watch she'd hurried away, the boy trailing disconsolately behind her. As Karen's train of followers flocked around his group, Adam stood aside. Karen came to him, hissing her indignation.

'Did you see that snooty woman drag her little boy away? I've been watching him. He was the one person out of the whole lot up there who was really listening.' Her voice rose angrily and several of the group looked up to nod agreement.

Adam imagined their reactions if he were to acknowledge the discriminating child as his son. He swallowed his disappointment but his determination strengthened to force a confrontation with Susannah that she could not walk away from. He watched the group of spectators hovering, most of them fascinated, round his group of players, trying to pick out the ones who had come to learn from the ones who merely wanted to display their wit.

They'd do well if they could produce a relevant quip that he had not heard before. In a minute, someone would notice the clothes pegs that stopped their music blowing away and would ask if they had brought their washing to dry. Simon was explaining that none of the instruments was original and that some of the musicians had made their own reproductions, his own effort being the hurdy-gurdy. He demonstrated how the handle turned against the string to make the drone, then lifted the long lid to show how the keys, when depressed, contacted the strings below it to play the tune.

The listeners were impressed. 'How long did it take you?'

Simon's answer was more precise than they had expected. 'A hundred and fifty hours.'

'Did that include chopping the tree down?' The musicians glared, as a man, at the would-be wit.

After a further ten minutes of admiring and explaining, a gangling and acne-scarred young man, who had turned up halfway through their frenetic race through 'All in a garden', suggested that the audience be treated to some more Playford. Adam's eyebrows rose. He didn't look the sort to recognize a collection of Renaissance dance tunes by name. He had loitered at the back of the crowd and then come forward to talk to Barry.

'Press,' Barry mouthed, moving towards Adam. 'Arrived late after lingering over his lunchtime pints. I don't think he wants to hear us but his brief is to get a picture of us playing.' Grateful for any publicity, the musicians resumed their seats.

'What are we doing?'

' "My Bonny Lass".'

Barry tutted in mock disapproval. 'Kindly leave the garden!'

Feeble wit must be catching. Adam sighed and removed a ladybird from his copy. The wind was getting up but the pegs held firm and no music flapped. As 'My Bonny Lass' proceeded, the wind got under the girls' skirts and they billowed like parachutes. Adam wondered if they might be taken up like God's chosen on the Last Day, leaving the unrepentant men still playing. The thought took him back to his student days. It was a text that that religious nut, Matt Hanson, was always quoting.

Suddenly the wind took the umbrella that was guarding the currently redundant instruments. Though the sun still glinted on the sackbut, there had been a distinct drop in temperature. Their fingers were stiffening and some of the runs and trills were suffering. It was not important; their audience was not discriminating.

The reporter was sitting where Karen had been, under the nearest apple tree, scribbling hard and ignoring them. Having listened long enough to decide which of his three or four standard sets of musical phrases best fitted their performance, he was writing it out from memory.

Karen had leapt up to rescue and re-anchor the umbrella and the crowd began to disappear. They played to the end of the piece, audienceless, feeling faintly silly. It was time for tea.

Wendy Allen, curator of Crossley Hall, was doing her mealtime stint at reception whilst Jane, her young assistant, took tea. When the hall was open the desk was always manned but she was rarely required to offer assistance. The general public and Jane Griffin seemed to take lunch and afternoon tea simultaneously. She was glad therefore to see Susannah and her young son approaching and anticipated a pleasant gossip. As they came nearer she registered the child's dejection and her friend's agitation.

She restricted her comment to the former. 'Didn't you enjoy the music, Luke?'

He nodded, casting a reproachful glance at his mother. Wendy reached across the counter and handed him the children's guide to the hall. He took it to the padded armchair by the entrance while she pulled out a stool beside her for Susannah. 'What's wrong with him? He's usually a little ray of sunshine.'

'I've just dragged him away when the band was offering to let the audience handle their instruments.' They both spoke in lowered voices, unsure whether Luke's bent head meant he was concentrating on the booklet or straining to hear his elders' conversation. 'And I've told him we might not make their concert tonight after all. When we leave here I'm taking my mother to the infirmary to visit Dad, so I've said we won't get away in time.'

'But why? You don't usually want to hang around the hospital – or at Julie's.'

Susannah lowered her voice still further. 'One of the musicians is Adam.'

'Adam? Adam *Holroyd*? In Yorkshire?'

Susannah nodded. 'In Yorkshire, in Cloughton, at Crossley Hall. He's seen us. And that's not all. I think

51

Urfan might be around too.' She described the incident that Luke had mentioned.

Wendy's eyes rounded. 'Oh Lord, Zannah, what are you going to do?'

Susannah parked in the neat, stone-faced terrace where her sister lived. Julie's house was conspicuous for its rather unkempt air. Its small front garden was bounded by privet hedges, on the left neatly trimmed by her neighbour and on the right a wild riot of summer growth. Princess Elizabeth roses were growing tall and healthy by the gate. They had not been dead-headed for some time so that the hips had become enormous and the flowers correspondingly small and ill-nourished. The effect was surprisingly attractive.

The earth in the small, sloping plot had been dug over, but weeds were squatting where flowers had failed to claim their rightful place. A pile of stones lay at the foot of the slope near the pavement. Her brother-in-law had obviously abandoned his plan to build a rockery. The nets in the bay window were crisp and clean but the white paintwork on the door less so. Still, this was a busy street and a bus route. Julie would need to wash the woodwork hourly to keep it free of greasy specks of soot.

Susannah felt sorry for Luke as he trailed up the path behind her. He had not been looking forward to this visit to his cousins, even before it had threatened to deprive him of his musical treat. Twelve-year-old Lisa tried to give him a rough, hands-on mothering that he found unacceptable, whilst the two boys, one a year older and one a year younger than him, indulged in vigorous horseplay that both scared and affronted him.

The two boys rushed to open the door, Wayne scowling when he saw who had rung the bell and Steven dribbling a football down the hall and kicking it violently through the open doorway, narrowly missing his cousin's head. Luke said hello and took a step nearer his mother. Both cousins ignored him, one galloping out to retrieve his ball and the other rapidly retreating upstairs.

Their mother came through from the living room and Susannah surveyed her. She wore no make-up as usual and her hair was roughly pulled back into a pony-tail. Luke was dispatched upstairs to play with Wayne. 'Make the most of it. You haven't long,' Susannah called after him to reassure him that his torture would not be prolonged.

The sisters went through to the living room and Susannah looked round impatiently. She could understand that Julie had little time for housework whilst their mother was taking up so much of her time, but how could she allow her family to create such a sordid mess in the first place?

Mother was sitting in an armchair in the corner. Susannah could see that even since her last visit the old woman had become thinner and looser about the mouth. Making no acknowledgement of her younger daughter's arrival, she continually lifted up the hem of her skirt, pleating it and revealing undergarments and flesh. Susannah was shocked. For most of her life, her mother had been on the prudish side of modest.

Julie was briskly cheerful. 'Come on, put your coat on, Mother.'

The old woman was indignant. 'I can't go out at this time of night!'

Julie reassured her. 'It's only half past five. Sue's taking you to the hospital to see Dad. Visiting begins at six.' Between them, the sisters inveigled flaccid arms into coat sleeves, their mother taking neither part nor interest in the proceedings.

'Why are we doing this?' Susannah asked, in an undertone. 'She won't remember that she's seen him.'

Julie shrugged. 'It's for Dad really.'

Susannah was not convinced. 'Do you think it will cheer him up to see her in this state?'

Julie silently fastened coat buttons whilst the old woman's fingers plucked at the lapels, then she turned. 'Take her for my sake then. It'll give me an hour or so to get something done without having to keep my eyes glued to her.'

Susannah nodded, acknowledging her sister's predicament. 'Does Kevin take her out?'

Julie's smile was mirthless. 'He would do but she's taken against him. If he's there she wants me there too to protect her from him. She's convinced he's taken all the money out of her purse and half the time she thinks Lisa's his fancy woman – says they ought to be ashamed of themselves.'

Suddenly, the old woman pulled herself to her feet, took Julie's arm and addressed Susannah. 'This lady is my daughter.' She regarded them both expectantly, apparently waiting for them to shake hands.

Susannah was horrified. 'Doesn't she know who I am?'

'I shouldn't think so. It's quite something that she's got me sorted out for once. Lisa!' Julie's daughter appeared from the adjoining kitchen. 'Can you take her to the loo before she goes?' Lisa nodded, approached her grandmother, got her attention by touching her arm, then beckoned. No word was spoken. When she left the room, the old woman followed. Julie smiled at Susannah. 'Lisa has a way with her. I couldn't cope without her. They understand each other. Mum can still manage when she actually gets there, thank goodness. By the way, you'll have to keep asking her if she wants to go whilst you're out. She won't mention it till it's too late.'

Susannah nodded. 'Does she know where the hospital cloakrooms are?'

Julie laughed. 'Sue, she doesn't know where *our* bathroom is and she's lived here nine weeks now.'

Appalled, Susannah went into the hall to call Luke down. She noted thankfully as he appeared that he was not crying. He looked more bored than scared. When she returned to the living room, she saw that her mother had taken her coat off again and dropped it in a heap on the floor.

As they eventually set off, Susannah, feeling slightly ashamed, told Luke to help his grandmother to the car. Doubtless it really would help to develop his sense of responsibility. It also obviated the need for her to touch the old woman's flesh. Her mother would clutch at her arm and she did not trust herself not to thrust her away.

She determined to keep the hospital visit as brief as possible. The evening concert at Crossley Hall, in spite of its attendant risks, was a much more bearable option.

Chapter Five

Susannah was glad she had decided to bring Luke to the evening concert after all. She hated breaking promises to him and to withdraw this treat would achieve nothing. Adam had already seen the child and there was no going back on it. She would just have to hope that he would not interfere now after having kept such a conveniently low profile for almost ten years. It occurred to her that she would have gone back on her word to anyone else without compunction if it had suited her purposes. A strong maternal instinct had not been the motive for her decision to go through with her pregnancy and keep her child, but he had become important to her. Maybe, in her own fashion, she even loved him.

He turned and grinned at her. The musicians were between pieces, the fattest of them delivering a lecturette. 'For medieval musicians, versatility was taken for granted . . .' She handed Luke a tube of peppermints and popped the one he offered her into her mouth. The fat man droned on ' . . . reed instruments loud enough to be played outdoors and flute-like ones for indoors . . .' He paused and invited the members of the group to demonstrate various sounds.

'Bass crumhorns and ducks make the same noise,' Luke whispered.

Eventually the fat man sat down and Adam got up to introduce the next set of pieces. 'To the courtiers of the Renaissance, dance was a serious art form as well as an entertainment. He or she would have been ashamed to take the floor at all if there was any doubt about his or her mastery of the art . . .'

Susannah soon ceased to take in the sense of the words, seduced by the well-modulated voice, the handsome head and the lean body. Maybe she should have settled for Adam – although it was only his body she had wanted and that was all she was attracted to now. She could never live with the whole man. It would mean a never-ending succession of evenings like tonight. Luke, beside her, was as fascinated by it all as she'd imagined he might be. He could not be understanding much of what Adam was saying but his concentration was intense. The instruments were taken up again but Susannah was not even sure whether they were playing the next pieces or just tuning up.

Adam was uncertain how well the performance was being received. The audience had listened politely through the first half and given restrained applause after their Floren-tine music and the fourteenth-century French songs. He had expected them to relax after the interval drinks and the lively, cheeky Playford Dances. His players were on form and no one could be finding fault with the manner of their execution. He had tried to loosen up their lis-teners with his 'Merry old England' spiel.

' . . . we may be shocked by the directness of these mostly three-hundred-year-old texts but they derive from an age before indoor plumbing and pooper-scooper laws. Everyday life was earthier . . .' Still they sat there, po-faced. Adam nodded to the instrumentalists to begin and hissed to his singers, 'Mime some drunken supping and give a few suggestive grunts and winks while we're waiting to come in.' They all gritted their teeth and embarked on what had been intended as a cheerful and rowdy finale. Slowly the audience began to respond. A few sniggers punctuated the music and the performers began to enjoy

57

themselves. Free to survey their listeners as he put in an ad-lib percussion, Adam saw that Susannah had left the hall.

He wasn't sure why she had come this evening. Had she changed her mind about introducing her son to him? And, surely she had not become so respectable and strait-laced in the last decade that she had departed as a protest at the vulgarity of their programme. The boy was still in his seat, eyes glued to the performers' dancing fingers, lips curved in a half smile. The smile, Adam was sure, marked his pleasure in the performance rather than an understanding of the innuendoes in the words of the songs. Even so, if Susannah was disgusted by what she was hearing she would surely have taken Luke with her.

The second half of the performance drew to an end at last. This time the applause was friendly and enthusiastic. Perhaps the group would be invited back after all. The usual invitation was issued to the listeners to handle the instruments which were laid out on a magnificent table, its top one slice from a huge tree trunk. Their audience surged forward and Adam, stepping back to make way for them, noticed the curator enter the hall and speak to his son. She had apparently suggested that he might like to join the crowd round the instruments and she now brought him forward. Adam led him to the far side of the table where his view was unimpeded and he could speak to the players.

The curator smiled her thanks. 'His mother was called away. She's bound to be back in a few minutes to pick him up. I said I'd keep an eye on him but I didn't expect her to be so long. Can I leave him here while I do my rounds?'

Adam answered with perfect honesty that he would be delighted to keep an eye on the boy.

As Luke carefully scrutinized the instruments laid out on the table, Adam carefully scrutinized him. Resentment rose in him against the mother. The monthly cheque that denied him the opportunity to expand his own musical activities was obviously just gilt on the gingerbread to Susannah. Her appearance seemed to have been metamorphosed by money. Her sexuality was less overtly displayed, and all the more effective for that. Maybe she had learned to dress with circumspection, but Adam thought rather that she was profiting from the good taste of the designers whose labels appealed to her and whose prices she could obviously now afford. He wondered if her appearance was a special effort to impress him but then remembered her little start of alarm when she had recognized him. He was sure that she had not expected to see him today. Besides, the chatter of his son, who was equally expensively clad, revealed an easy acceptance of their affluence.

The boy picked up a recorder. 'Are these old?'

Adam took it from him to demonstrate. 'It depends on what you mean. In medieval times there were various kinds of pipes and some were like recorders. They had a beak-shaped mouthpiece and seven finger-holes. But Robert made these for us. Do you play a recorder at school?' The boy nodded shyly and Adam could see that his fingers itched. 'Let's hear you.'

Luke hesitated, eyeing the remnants of the evening's audience nervously. 'I can't play like you did.'

'Neither could I when I was nine.'

'How did you know I was nine?'

Adam distracted him by handing him the easiest of the sheets of music in the folder and setting it on a stand. Thus encouraged, the boy began to play, haltingly at first. Then, as the tune pleased him, he let it take over and forgot his audience. Adam was thrilled. The piece was very easy but this small boy was aware of its possibilities. As he reached the last bar, everyone in the room applauded him. He showed no embarrassment but merely asked, 'How do you make it sound like a bird singing?'

Adam showed him how to play a trill, vowing that from

59

now on Susannah's edict no longer held sway. He would claim his right to have access to this delightful son. Luke had transferred his attention to a shawm.

'It made me jump when you blew that this afternoon.'

Adam was surprised and fiercely proud that his son had separated out the sound of one instrument from the consort. He began to explain the simultaneous sucking and blowing required to produce a sound from it. His cheeks bulging, the child solemnly blew and sucked alternately for some seconds before shaking his head. 'I can't do it.'

'I shouldn't worry. I can only do it sometimes and I've been practising ever since I knew your mother at university.'

It was obvious that Susannah had not mentioned their previous acquaintance to him. He absorbed the idea, then asked, 'Did you know my father too?'

Adam floundered. 'Well, sort of . . .'

'He died before I was even a baby.'

A spurt of anger suffused Adam. Suddenly he hated Susannah. She had prevented him understanding the privilege of being a father. Now he understood, he intended to enjoy it. Besides, there was no way the Susannah he had known could give this boy what he needed. 'Do you have music lessons other than at your school recorder club?'

The child shook his head regretfully. 'My mother says when I'm older.'

Adam's hackles rose. She was denying the boy the air he needed to breathe. If he wanted to be a professional musician he should have begun on some instrument a couple of years ago – not that he despised the recorder, of course. The school music teacher seemed not to be squashing Luke's enthusiasm or letting him develop a sloppy technique, but was doing little else besides. He'd tackle Susannah tonight.

Instruments seemed to have disappeared from the

table. Adam became aware that the rest of his party faced the prospect of a through-the-night drive south and were impatiently waiting to pack up. He hastily applied himself whilst Luke watched with continued interest. He sat quietly on the front row of chairs as farewells were said and the musicians departed. Adam saw that, as a result of a couple of innocently ambiguous remarks and many shared glances, Karen had managed to get left behind.

Luke came forward and politely resumed their conversation. 'We came here last Wednesday to have a preview of all the exhibitions. We had to take off all our uniforms and wear old-fashioned clothes. The girls liked it but I felt a bit stupid. Do you feel stupid dressed like that?'

Adam considered. 'Not whilst we're playing, but I sometimes do afterwards.'

He noticed the curator had come through from her office. She looked anxious as she approached. 'You haven't been left behind because of Luke, have you? I'm sure Susannah didn't mean to be so late.'

Adam explained his intention of staying overnight in Cloughton and asked if she could recommend a suitable small hotel. With an appraising glance at Karen, she obliged.

Adam ignored the glance and thanked her. 'If you have any more duties, do please get on with them. I'm sure Luke's mother won't be long and he's entertaining me very well in the meantime.'

Luke resumed the entertainment with a smile, pointing over his shoulder. 'Do you know what's under the lime-wash on that wall?' Adam exhibited the required ignorance. 'It's daub and it's made of sand and straw and cow flops.' His tone lent the last words a couple of exclamation marks. 'It's called wattle and daub construction. Our teacher told us about it.'

Adam took the opportunity to ask about his school. He was not surprised to discover it was fee-paying and of

61

some repute. He had realized that Luke's cultured way of speaking had not been picked up at the local primary. Luke was keen to go on sharing his recently acquired knowledge. 'The family put that bay window in to show they were very rich. Glass was very expensive and they could only make it in little pieces. They had to use those lead strips to hold it together. And have you seen the knot garden? It's got a very funny sign that says "Please walk on the grass and keep off the gravel paths".'

'You've been listening very hard.'

He listened hard to himself. How should a father talk to his nine-year-old son? Did he sound patronizing? He was glad for some time to observe him as Karen began to chat to the child. He sought in vain for any echo of his own features. Luke was fair-haired and blue-eyed like both parents, but in most other respects was the image of Susannah.

He watched the small, animated face and was irritated when the curator interrupted again. Her tone was apologetic. 'You've been very good but I can't impose on you any longer.' She lowered her voice and half turned her back on the child, who politely looked away. 'I'm feeling quite worried. Susannah stretched a point for tonight's concert but Luke's bedtime is sacrosanct. If she'd been held up somewhere, she'd have let me know.'

Adam was sceptical. 'She wasn't always so solicitous of people's feelings . . .'

'Of course, you knew her . . .'

'Did she tell you about that?'

Wendy Allen looked uneasy at Adam's eager response. 'She just mentioned that she'd been at university with one of you. I suggest now that you ring your hotel from here to avoid a possible wasted journey and then get off. I'll leave a note on the door for when Susannah gets back here, then I'll take the lad home with me for the night. She can pick him up in the morning. If she's much longer, I'll seriously think about ringing the police.'

Adam reluctantly agreed to this plan. As he left the hall grounds and turned into the main road he did not meet ex-girl guide Vanessa Smith. She had completed her Good Samaritan act some half hour earlier.

Chapter Six

Detective Constable Jennie Taylor's driving, as she left Cloughton Royal Hospital, was adversely affected by the vexation she felt, a reprehensible fault in the wife of a sergeant in traffic division, but understandable, she thought, in the circumstances.

'Her' rape victim, whose plight had kept Jennie busy for most of her shift the previous day, had regained consciousness just before five o'clock this Sunday morning. In accordance with instructions, the sister of ward 6 had rung Jennie's number and Jennie had arrived post-haste at the victim's bedside, only to find she had relapsed into her coma. The long-anticipated lie-in had been forfeited to no purpose and the telephone had woken fifteen-month-old Lucy. Jennie did not relish serving breakfast to a husband and daughter of whom neither had had their sleep out.

Half a mile from home, as she was passing the grounds of Crossley Hall, she became aware of a disturbance at the bus shelter. A middle-aged man in working overalls flagged down her car, whilst his younger companion supported a half-fainting girl. She wound down her passenger window and the overalled man stuck his head into the car.

'Don't get out, love. I wouldn't like you to see what's in there. Young woman's had a nasty accident, or been the victim of an attack, more like. Could you drive on to the next telephone and get us the police and an ambulance?'

Grimly, Jennie showed him her warrant card before driving the car safely beyond the bus stop and climbing out. Quickly establishing that the languishing girl was merely a witness to rather than the recipient of the reported injuries, she went into the shelter from the side farthest from the road and bent over the figure that lay on the ground. The victim was flat on her back, surrounded by slivers of glass from a broken pane, her head propped up against a red-painted metal panel.

A few seconds' scrutiny established, at least to Jennie's own satisfaction, that life was extinct. Nevertheless, she summoned an ambulance before calling headquarters for instructions. None of the three would-be bus passengers could offer much information and after noting names, addresses and the purpose of their early-morning journeys, Jennie offered the girl the back seat of her car to lie on, whilst the two men squatted on the pavement, happy to have an excuse for not arriving at the service station on the M62 for the beginning of their shift.

Standing where all three of them were in sight, Jennie looked down again at the body. It was clad in a light wool suit in silver-grey. The pleated skirt finished above the knee and the jacket reached down almost to its hem. Jennie knew her fashion. The labels were tucked out of sight but she thought they would probably say 'Gucci', and if she were to look for the garments in the relevant catalogue, it would have to be the current year's.

She was struck by the contrast between the designer clothes and the surrounding litter. For some odd reason, it was more shocking to see a Gucci jacket smeared with the dog excrement into which the body had slipped than to see the gaping neck wound from which the young woman seemed to have bled to death.

She could see surprisingly little blood-staining on the jacket, and had a sudden, macabre vision of the victim, in her death throes, frantically trying to avoid bleeding on her best suit. She tried to suppress a hysterical giggle and realized she was in shock. Not that the sight of a dead body was a new experience, but in six years of CID work she had not previously been the first officer on the scene. Perhaps she could forgive herself this unseemly reaction. She had never before scrutinized a messy death so closely, or felt so responsible.

She stepped out of the shelter, took a deep breath and bumped into Dr Stocks. She left him to comply with the law by pronouncing the corpse dead, cancelled the ambulance she had called and looked around her.

The sordid scene was neatly contained in this vandalized box of glass and metal. Outside it, the rest of the world was still beautiful. It was not yet sufficiently light for the autumn foliage to glow. The trees bordering the grounds of Crossley Hall were black silhouettes, clean, still shapes against the shifting streaks of gold on blue that promised the sun's imminent arrival on the skyline; the passing cars were still vague dark shapes behind a dazzle of passing headlights.

A van drew up in front of her own car and the men who emerged from it began to set up a temporary bus stop a hundred yards nearer town and to cordon off the permanent shelter. She raised her hand in greeting to an assortment of her husband Paul's colleagues. She was thankful when the next vehicle to arrive contained Chief Inspector Browne and Ledgard, the pathologist.

The CI was delighted to be called into service so early this morning. After weeks of hints, delicate and indelicate, from his son that his narrow silhouette did not in necessarily bespeak low blood cholesterol or peak fitness, he had agreed to a trial jog round the force's football pitches before breakfast. To have Alex back in Cloughton might prove a mixed blessing – going on duty was the one excuse that both he and Hannah would countenance.

He could see that Jennie did not share his satisfaction and that she had found the sole company of a messy corpse a trial. He chatted inconsequentially for a minute to give her time to adjust to her usual role as a member of his team. 'Started the inventory, have you? Grey suit, white shirt-blouse . . .' Jennie elaborated on this description and Browne nodded. 'Yes, I can see they don't come from M and S. Pity the scarf got bloody and disarranged.'

'Why?'

Browne shrugged. 'As far as dress is concerned, there are two sorts of women – those who wear a scarf to keep their necks warm and those who use it to turn a random collection of garments into a co-ordinated outfit, the shape right, the colours right. This girl's one of the latter, I think.' So was Hannah, Browne's wife. Jennie was amused as Browne looked round the shelter carefully. 'No handbag. Car keys on the floor. I wonder if they fit that Alfa Romeo parked beyond the double yellows.'

Jennie thought it unlikely. 'Why get out of a posh car to go into a bus shelter?'

'To offer someone a lift?'

'Wouldn't you just stop right beside it and open your passenger door? You wouldn't get nicked for only stopping long enough to let somebody in.'

Browne nodded and stood back to make way for the photographer. 'Ask your SOCO brothers to deal with those keys first, would you?' Already clicking and flashing, the man nodded and Browne wandered off to talk to the discoverers of the body. The two men had watched developments with a lively interest and were reluctant, when they had told what little they knew, to accept the offer of a lift on to the motorway in a police van.

The girl had soon recovered enough to sit up and look through Jennie's car window but she suffered an elaborate relapse when work was mentioned and contrived to be sent home instead.

When Browne returned to the bus shelter, the photographer had disappeared and Ledgard was squatting awkwardly by the body in an attempt to avoid the broken glass. He was obviously not yet ready to divulge his findings, but offered over his shoulder, 'Pearson says that Alfa isn't locked.' As Browne was sure the pathologist had intended, he wandered away with Jennie to inspect it. The less the pathologist was harried, the more he would get out of him. He would amuse himself elsewhere until the clinical examination of the body was complete.

The sun, he noticed, had almost made it to the horizon and the garden hedges they passed were festooned with glittering webs. He supposed they were always there but it took these particular conditions to decorate them so that they caught his attention. He liked autumn. It was a time when he could relax and be slovenly because nature herself was being untidy.

His DC brought him down to earth. 'It must be her car, sir. She's not wearing a coat so she didn't intend to be out in the open for more than a minute. And it's unlocked because she'd be keeping it in sight.'

Browne nodded as they came alongside the vehicle and stood staring at it. It was a discreet dark green, inside and out, recently washed and immaculate. Its registration was for the previous year and its tyres were new. An unemployed steering-wheel lock lay on the front passenger seat and a small clutch-type handbag was on the floor. Browne put on the thin rubber gloves he had carried in his pocket and opened the bag, levering up the press-stud fastener with a penknife.

'It's a decorative affair,' Jennie observed, peering at it. 'Not an evening bag exactly, but not a serviceable, everyday carry-all that would tell us a lot about her. It's definitely expensive. The purse is pretty, but that's not practical either.' The purse, however, contained a snapshot of the dead girl with a fair-haired boy which provided Browne's justification for his search of the vehicle.

He looked at his DC hopefully. 'I know you're officially off-duty, Jennie, but could you help for a while? Benny's taken Virginia and the child to visit his eldest sister in St Albans for the weekend. I've called him back early but he'll be a couple of hours yet. Jerry will be along soon but Annette's not well.'

Jennie sighed, then accepted the second pair of rubber gloves he was tentatively offering. Browne smiled his thanks as she pulled them on. 'There was obviously no attack in the car. Whoever did it probably went no nearer here than the bus shelter but we'd better take no risks.' He was anxious to get back to the body and was confident that the girl would search competently.

Leaving Ledgard to his own devices paid dividends. He was happy to communicate such facts as he had established as soon as Browne had sympathized with his catalogue of aches and pains, caused by the draughty shelter and the awkward stance he had had to adopt to prevent both knees being sliced.

Browne pointed to the smashed pane above the girl's head. A large, jagged splinter, liberally bloodied, was still firmly fixed in the metal frame. 'Is that what did the damage?'

Ledgard nodded. 'That seems a sensible assumption. Its edges are sharp and the gash in the neck is a clean-cut, surgical type of wound.'

Browne circled the shelter, examining the glass spike from the outside before coming back in to ask, 'Is this an accident? Could the other participant in this scuffle have left without knowing how grave the injury was?'

Ledgard shook his head. 'The jugular vein is severed. The blood wouldn't have sprayed like it does from an artery but the bleeding would be copious and immediate. It would well up and run down to the under-surfaces of the body. The scarf partly contained it until she collapsed.'

Their eyes followed the dark trail of tacky blood just discernible on the brighter red paint of the metal panel below the broken pane. 'Then it made a pool on the pavement.'

'And soaked into the jacket and skirt beneath the body. So, is it our pigeon?'

He was asking himself but Ledgard ventured an

opinion. 'At the very least, I think she was left to die. I suppose you want to know when. Her temperature has dropped nine degrees C. She's been here all night but it wasn't cold for October, lividity is marked, rigor's reached the arms and trunk but the legs are still floppy. You know the amount of leeway I need at this stage but, for now, you can take nine thirty as a working hypothesis.'

He began to replace equipment in his bag. 'By the way, there's a long gash in the back of her upper arm too. Two serious wounds in different locations would seem to me to preclude an accident.'

Chapter Seven

At nine o'clock, the time Browne's team usually assembled in his office, he sat there alone. His son-in-law had telephoned from his car. After getting his recall, he had departed from his sister's house just as soon as Virginia could pack, but now they were held up by road-works on the M1.

Jennie had hurried home to feed her family. She'd looked worried. Browne didn't know Paul's shifts but he did know the effect of CID work on family life. Hannah and he had weathered it, using a formula they had hammered out between them, which would serve as a blueprint for nobody else. Jennie and Paul would have to do likewise. Benny and Virginia were lucky. His daughter had at least had her eyes wide open when she had chosen to marry a policeman. Jerry and Annette seemed to cope well enough too.

The thought prompted him to consult his watch. What was Jerry doing? As if on cue, his sergeant tapped at the door and came in. When Browne enquired after Annette, he looked sheepish. 'It'll take her seven months or so to recover.'

Browne grinned delightedly. Jerry had obviously learned to combine his work and his home life very efficiently. 'You old devil! I bet Fliss is thrilled.'

Hunter pulled a plastic chair towards him and settled facing its back. 'As only a twelve-year-old could be. Amazingly, so is Annette.'

Browne filled Hunter in with details of the new case until the telephone rang. He heard the voice of Bennett from the desk in the station foyer. Wendy Allen was proving a persistent caller. 'She rang last night, sir, before her friend had been missing three hours. It's not as if she's a vulnerable adult. I'm sorry to bother you with it.'

But Browne was interested. 'Go on.'

'Well, the boy's a complication, you see. She's not likely just to have dumped him. Miss Allen kept him for the night but she has to open the hall this morning so she's taken him with her – very worried because he's in yesterday's dirty clothes, and she doesn't know whether to ring the boy's aunt. Doesn't want to worry her unnecessarily. Apparently she's got worries enough of her own.'

Browne covered the mouthpiece and gestured to Hunter to put his coat back on. 'Looks like we might have an identification already.' He turned back to the telephone. 'Tell her I'm sending somebody.'

Hunter paused at the door. 'Did you get anything from the car?'

'Not a lot. A sort of evening bag, a child's book, unmarked. The boot was locked. The keys were beside the body but dabs have them, I'll wait a bit longer if we can get details from a witness instead. I don't like breaking into things.'

'And what are our orders from on high?'

'Our respected super has issued his standard instruction. "Treat it as foul play for the moment but keep it low-key." I offer my equally standard translation. "Do your own thing. If it's a storm in a teacup and we've investigated it in detail, we'll carry the can for wasting time and money. If it's murder and we haven't done enough, we have our hands slapped for being slack." Either way, Petty's egg ends up on our faces.' Hunter shrugged and closed the door behind him.

Browne smiled to himself as the sergeant's footsteps retreated down the corridor. So, the Hunters were breed-

ing again after a twelve-year rest. He hoped Jerry was
going to be able to keep his mind on the job.

Hunter was a frequent visitor to Crossley Hall. This morning he indulged himself by approaching the house through
the knot garden and observing the different geometrical
designs on the black and white wood and plaster of the
house's south face, as his children had done countless
times in the past. Then he wended his familiar way
through the Long Gallery, enjoying the reassuring sense
of permanence emanating from the massive old timbers of
the beams and the floorboards, before descending the
main stairway to the entrance hall. Here he enjoyed
the leaded and pebble-glassed windows and ignored the
modern reception desk.

Wendy Allen recognized his face and looked startled.
'Hello again.' She was polite but firm. 'I'm afraid we
aren't officially open till eleven. How did you get in that
way?'

Hunter came forward and offered his warrant card.
'With this. It seems we can help you.'

She forgot her problem in her surprise. 'You're a policeman? But . . .'

Hunter smiled at her. 'You thought coppers wore hel-
mets and kicked doors in rather than admire the carving
on them?'

She recovered from her confusion by enquiring after
his children. 'Fliss is fine. I expect she'll be along here
again at half-term. Tim's a sixth-former now. Thinks he
has better things to do.'

They regarded one another in silence for a moment,
Hunter wondering whether the woman's portly figure in
longish dark skirt and demure sprigged blouse, and her
long hair neatly knotted at the nape, were meant to be
'in period', part of the value offered for the price of the
entrance ticket. He tried to imagine her in a restaurant,
shopping in the town precinct, tried and failed to see her

73

at a party or theatre with the young woman in the snap-shot in his pocket. He drew it out and handed it to her. 'Is this your missing friend?'

She glanced at it and nodded. 'Where did you get it?' Her face told Hunter that she knew the answer would be bad news.

She listened impassively as he gave it, considered it for some seconds, then remarked, 'Luke is assuming his mother has been called out on a job. I haven't disillusioned him.'

'Where is he now?'

She pointed through the ornate, carved doorway that led to the main rooms. 'In the Great Hall. I've given him some boxes of postcards and pamphlets to sort out. The visitors take a positive delight in muddling them up, especially the ones who don't buy any.' Hunter was unsure whether this chatter was to mask her shock and grief or whether it meant she was feeling neither. At least Luke merited an indulgent smile. 'What he's really doing is reliving last night's concert and trying to think of a way of wangling another meeting with the player who talked to him whilst I was clearing up and doing the rounds.'

'What was his name?'

She hesitated, then said, 'Adam something.' She seemed reluctant to admit even so much.

'Had you met him before?' She shook her head. 'So, why were you willing to trust him with the boy?' She shrugged as though she had been asking herself the same question. Hunter moved on. 'M/s Farrar was not wearing a wedding ring. Who is her next of kin, besides her son?'

'Her parents, I suppose – and she has an older sister.'

Hunter was noting the required details when the boy appeared, tiny in the massive doorway, carefully carrying his box of sorted cards. His face lit up as he caught a side view of Hunter's tall spare form and fair head. Dropping the cards on the desk he came forward eagerly. His face fell a little as he approached before he offered his hand politely to the sergeant. 'Hello. Sorry, I thought you were Mr Holroyd.'

Hunter shook hands solemnly as the curator went across to unlock the door leading to the modern kitchen and cafeteria. She turned to Luke. 'Could you put the kettle on for us? I'll come when it boils.'

The boy was offended. 'I can make coffee. I do at home.' He disappeared, closing the door.

'And his father?' Hunter asked, quietly.

She coloured. 'Someone Susannah knew as a student. She got pregnant in her last term.'

'And his name and address?'

She blushed again. 'I don't know where he lives. She didn't tell me. She doesn't – didn't – see him.' Hunter waited for more but she glared at him, resolutely silent.

Temporarily, he relinquished the point. 'You mentioned a job that Luke thinks she's busy with. What did she do for a living?'

Now Miss Allen was anxious to elaborate. 'It wasn't one job, it was several. She was in the process of setting up a literary agency. She liked the idea of reaping profits from clients for up to fifty years after they'd died. I think she was having a go at writing her own book – there's part of a novel on the stocks somewhere – and she was toying with the idea of launching a magazine, though even Zannah would have had to settle for one or the other eventually if they'd both taken off in a big way.

'After university, with Luke as a baby, she began with freelance proof reading and copy editing that she could do at home, and, after a year or so, she became UK correspondent for a couple of foreign publications, one in Germany and one in France. She wrote about the English theatre for them. She'd heard that it would pay for some overseas travel and it did. She left Luke with Julie at first when she had to go away, and occasionally with me, but recently she's taken him with her.'

She stopped, having reached the end of what struck Hunter as a carefully prepared statement. He let the silence lengthen and her unease increase. She looked into his face anxiously. 'They were all jobs where you could arrange your timetable to suit yourself, and start with minimal equipment, just a telephone and a typewriter and some paper, but where being pushy gave you an edge.'

'So she was pushy?'

Wendy Allen nodded. 'She had to be her own boss. She was very attractive, extremely good company, but she was a manipulator. She wasn't fond of advice and she was totally resistant to influence or control.' Hunter tried the silence again but she had retreated, ostensibly to check Luke's sorting of the cards.

'You described yourself as her friend. An unblinkered one, apparently.'

She nodded. 'I never expected Zannah to do anything for me in exchange for what I did for her. She liked that. I enjoyed her wit and an occasional trip into her frenzied lifestyle. I couldn't have coped with it full time. I enjoy the peace here, being steeped in the past, but a night out with Zannah was stimulating. We did things together but we weren't close. She didn't need or want any commitment, but she required a companion now and then, for the sake of appearing to have a friend.'

There was a resounding crash from the kitchen. So much for Luke's coffee-making talents. They reached the door together but the child was unharmed. He had merely dropped the tray of cups and saucers, sugar and milk, in his struggle with an unyielding doorknob. He bent to gather up the shards of pottery and Miss Allen addressed the top of his shamed head. 'Can you remind me, Luke, to get that handle fixed tomorrow? I did just the selfsame thing as you one day last week.'

After a few further words, Hunter left her, happy that *she* was going to be the one to inform the child of his mother's death.

*

76

Hunter was entering the dimness of the Yew Tunnel, taking, as a final self-indulgence, the long way round back to the car park, as Adam Holroyd rolled over, half awake, and pinched himself hard. When his eyes had stopped watering, he could still see Karen's head on the pillow beside him. He took a deep breath and let it out slowly, remembering the previous night in small patches which gradually grew larger until they merged in total recall.

It had all been so straightforward. He had asked, 'Are you coming with me?' and she had nodded. Their decision to take a double room had been equally simple, and then they had made love like an old married couple, with mutual satisfaction and no discussion. Even Zannah, who always went straight for what she wanted with no deviation, had taken longer to seduce him. Not that Karen had seduced him, nor he her. They had merely made a fuss-free decision to be together.

In post-coital intimacy, they had talked easily about Luke and about Karen's chemotherapy, six years ago, that had left her sterile. They were satisfied, having shared the facts, to leave the ramifications till later.

Not for the first time, he wondered why Zannah had wanted to sleep with him all those years ago. She had liked him, perhaps, but she certainly had not loved him. And yet, he thought, it had been something other than pure lust that had smouldered, temporarily, between them. She had refused to let him meet her family and he had not been able to imagine what kind of home she had come from. Her attitudes and priorities were such an incongruous mixture.

The bed creaked and Karen opened her eyes. He banished all thoughts of Susannah.

Chapter Eight

From Crossley Hall, Hunter drove downhill towards the
centre of Cloughton, on his way calling on Wendy Allen's
young assistant, Jane, for an unproductive few minutes.
She had taken the telephone call summoning Susannah
Farrar away from the concert but had recalled nothing
about it that was any use to him. At the roundabout
below the police station he was held up by a long queue
of vehicles.

He waited philosophically, wondering where the motor-
ists were bound. No shops were open in the precinct and
they were going in the wrong direction for the Sunday
market. The only place open for business at this end of
town was All Saints, the old parish church of Cloughton
when it had been just a village. Hunter had a sudden
picture of all the drivers before him fighting for parking
places alongside the churchyard and shoving one another
aside in an attempt to appropriate the last few pew spaces
before the baize-lined doors swung to, shutting out would-
be worshippers.

He banished this unlikely vision, realizing that for this
morning the choir of St Oswald's would be singing their
anthem without his own useful tenor. The cars in front
were still stationary and he turned his attention to the
almost-aerial view of the bus station downhill to his right.
The town amenities were collected together in the hollow
that was Cloughton. Deep greyish-greenish-brownish
slabs of hillside surrounded it on three sides, containing

78

it and saving it from developing into a sprawling city.

For the first time, Hunter thought that maybe the bus station deserved the prize for design that it had won several years ago. On the rare occasions that he had gone into it, he had been in the wake of some accessory to a crime, but from here, he could admire the metal-vaulted roof, airy and graceful, the gleaming panes between the ribs forming the sort of pattern you saw through a kaleidoscope.

Suddenly, the car in front began to move. Hunter followed, reaching the roundabout and swinging without further delay into the main road that soon began to climb the other side of the valley. The house where Susannah Farrar had lived was on a quiet side street, about three-quarters of a mile from the town centre.

The estate agents who advertised in the *Clarion* described all the houses in Crossley Bridge as 'exclusive'. The small ones were 'bijou, miniature, diminutive', the big words compensating for the small meaning. The larger ones had rooms that were 'spacious', storage was 'commodious' and lawns were 'expansive'.

Hunter parked outside number five, Clough View, which was something in between, though detached with a pretentious garden. Very recently, he had drastically revised his idea of the ideal garden – easy maintenance and small size losing precedence in favour of space to park a pram again, re-erect the swing and kick a ball around. Susannah Farrar seemed to have considered it as a decorative setting for her house and he doubted whether the close-shaven lawns and colourful borders were the results of her own sweated labour. He thought a landscape gardener might make a very comfortable living in these parts.

It occurred to him that Browne must have been here for some time now and he hurried inside to meet him. It was not Browne's voice that he heard as the door opened, however. 'And, after all that there was another dirty great queue at the Bradholme roundabout.' Hunter could bear witness to that! So, the M1 had yielded Mitchell up to them.

The CI turned from his son-in-law to greet his sergeant. 'Morning, Jerry.' His eyes twinkled. 'I never thought the day would come, but it seems you two have something in common at last. Temporarily, at least.'

The two younger officers regarded one another, puzzled. Mitchell was stocky, blunt-featured and brash. Hunter, six feet four inches, was thin and bookish. Under Browne's authority, they had taunted and provoked one another until a grudging regard for each other's very different talents had taught them to live together fairly amicably. Light dawned on Mitchell first and his face registered astonishment, then amusement.

'Well, we still have Declan's first-size things put away. It's going to prove an expensive impulse for you.'

Hunter scowled. Three years ago, Mitchell had impregnated Browne's daughter just a short while before marrying her. The sergeant had uttered no taunts, swallowed his disapproval and wished the couple well.

Mitchell remembered and offered his hand. 'We'll save the mutual congratulations till we get to the pub.'

Hunter shook it, then turned to Browne. 'I got nowhere with the phone call. Apparently it was just a brief request for Miss Farrar to be brought to the phone. It was either a high-voiced man or a low-voiced woman and a bad line – that or a lot of noise at both ends. The band could be heard at the hall, of course. She couldn't remember what the background to the voice was and when Miss Farrar spoke to the caller she can't remember much of what was said. She wasn't really listening – if you can believe that – but at one point Miss Farrar told her caller not to be melodramatic.'

Browne shrugged. 'Did Miss Allen have anything to tell you?'

'Quite a lot. She's a very articulate lady. She wrote the

guide book they sell at the hall and she's done a proper book on the history of the original family. Even so . . .'

'Yes?'

Hunter wrinkled his nose, trying to analyse his dissatisfaction with this witness. 'Everything she told me was worked out and neatly tabulated. Even if you write books you don't usually talk in well-constructed paragraphs unless you've been practising. It was as if she had suspected there would be an enquiry into all this. She went into great detail about Miss Farrar's career – gave me a regular CV. I got the impression she was trying to keep me from asking about something else.'

'Such as?'

'Such as who the child's father is.'

Mitchell had been quiet for too long. 'So you think the killer is the boy's father?'

Hunter shook his head impatiently. 'I didn't say that – but I think that might be what Miss Allen thinks.'

Browne, who had made himself familiar with the house, showed them round briefly and proprietorially. 'Luke has a playroom as well as his own bedroom.' He opened a door at the end of the hall on the ground floor.

Mitchell took a step inside and whistled. 'Make a list of the things this poor child's deprived of and we'll order some in.' The boy seemed to have his own TV set and video recorder. Recordings for it were stacked on bookshelves which ran the length of one of the narrower walls, as far up as a child could reach. They included children's classics and wildlife films and only two American cartoons. Books filled the rest of the shelves.

Hunter saw Tolkien and Kipling, *Watership Down* and *Alice*, *Just William* and a host of attractive paperbacks. He picked up a handful and approved. They were well treated and also well thumbed. Drawers and cupboards yielded a chess set, a simple camera, a small microscope. Hunter nodded at Mitchell's comment but added, 'I rather think, from what I heard, that he'd prefer a musical instrument to any of this. I wonder what the mother's bookcase contains.'

'Go into the sitting room and look.' Browne made off up the hall. 'At the moment I'm more interested in her diary and answering machine and the rest of the paraphernalia in here.' He opened a door. 'This room was double locked when I arrived, so there's something either confidential or valuable for us to find.' He disappeared, shutting the door behind him, only to shoot out again a few seconds later as the phone rang. 'Don't answer it.'

PC Caroline Webster came in from sentry duty outside as he added, more politely, 'I want a woman to answer it. If the caller hears a woman's voice . . .'

'He or she might think it's the girl herself . . .'

'You're way ahead of me,' Browne told his son-in-law with a tight smile. As the answering machine clicked on, the PC picked up the receiver. Browne carefully lifted the one in the office, this time leaving the door open.

Obeying instructions, the PC waited until the machine had given out its brief message, then said a breathless 'Hello' over the end of it. The machine recorded the message, amplifying it so that they could all hear. 'It's Adam, Zannah. I found your number in the directory. I don't know where you got to last night but I'm not leaving here until we've talked about the boy.'

'The boy?' the PC echoed.

'Don't mess me about, Zannah. I'm mad not to have demanded access before. I've maintained him as best I could so I've a right to see him. I said nothing last night. The poor child needs preparing for me but we got on well. I don't think he'll be disappointed. And don't shout me down like you used to . . .' It apparently occurred to the caller that no shouting was going on. 'Are you listening?'

Briefly the PC asked, 'Where are you?'

They could hear the pleased surprise in the caller's voice as he offered the name of his hotel. 'Do you want to come round, or shall I come to you?'

82

'We'll come.'

Adam's voice was anxious. 'Don't bring Luke till we've worked something out. Can you leave him with someone?'

'Yes.'

'Are you coming right away?'

'Yes.'

The PC replaced the receiver. 'Phew! Nearly blew it at the end, sir.'

Browne let out his sharply indrawn breath. 'Never mind, you did well. You extracted all we need and risked less than a dozen words. Like to go with Jerry and confess to him?'

The PC laughed and she and Hunter obediently set off for the hotel.

After a cursory inspection of the ground floor, Mitchell wandered into the office where Browne had returned to his search. 'This case is like a treasure hunt,' he announced. 'Follow up the first clue properly and along comes the second.'

Browne turned round, a satisfied smile on his face. 'And the third.' He handed over the sheaf of bank statements he was holding in his hand.

The Three Ravens Hotel was medium sized, respectable and unpretentious. It was on the same road as, and about a quarter of a mile from, the already notorious bus shelter where Susannah's body had been found. The area of pavement in front of it was shielded from the elements by a wrought-iron and glass canopy from which flowering baskets were suspended. The fuchsia and geraniums had almost finished their summer blossoming and the remaining flowers seemed bleached and faded. Greyish-green foliage that Hunter could not name trailed untrimmed, and brushed against his face. He found the pastel colours restful, after the burning red and gold of the October foliage, which always took him by surprise with its un-British flamboyancy. This year, he realized, there had as

83

yet been no autumn gales and the riot of autumn colours had been unusually prolonged.

Knowing that the receptionist would have been told to expect a female visitor, Hunter sent PC Webster to report to her. 'I'll wait for you by the stairs, Caroline, instead of the lift, then she won't see us together and ring to warn him.' PC Webster obtained the room number and they hurried together up to the second floor.

His first glimpse of Adam Holroyd aroused all Hunter's prejudices. The man was the sort who got music and musicians a bad name. His hair hung below his collar and he wore a sort of yellow, polo-necked T-shirt, much washed and out of shape. This was Sunday, for goodness' sake. Hunter supposed the hair might offend even more in combination with a suit and the man's face did look clever and sensitive. It was like a camel's, all bones and long white eyelashes. Hunter liked animals and this comparison did a great deal to counteract the unfavourable first impression. There was a fair-haired girl in the room behind him. Even though the child's mother was expected, she wore the young man's pyjama jacket and nothing else. Obviously Holroyd was not demanding access to the boy in the hope of renewing his relationship with Susannah. When she saw Hunter the girl dived into the adjoining bathroom.

Caroline Webster displayed her credentials and apologized to the young man for her impersonation. He looked puzzled rather than affronted. 'But why? Where's Zannah? . . . It explains the accent, though.'

Caroline frowned. 'But my accent's local.'

'Yes, hers wasn't. She dropped it years ago, part of shaking the dust of the past off her feet when she got away to university.'

'She came back, though.'

He shrugged. 'Well, it's a beautiful little town and I suppose she could be "refined" here as well as anywhere.' He stressed the adjective, making it derogatory. 'Her clothes had become up-market so I thought it unlikely she had abandoned the Oxbridge vowels.' He recollected himself and frowned. 'Why are you here?'

Hunter displaycd his own warrant card, then walked past the young man into his room and put it on a small table.

Adam followed him. 'What's going on? Is Zannah not coming? I haven't come to break anything up – as you can see, I'm already very well provided for.' He turned and realized Karen was missing. Almost immediately she came out of the bathroom, fully clothed.

Hunter sat in an armchair. 'Look, I haven't met Miss Farrar but I am here in connection with her and I am on duty. Please answer my questions and afterwards I'll answer at least some of yours.'

Adam took another glance at Hunter's warrant card, then watched Caroline settle herself on an upright chair beside the bed to take notes. At Hunter's prompting, he described briefly the history of his relationship with Susannah and the circumstances of his being in Cloughton this weekend.

Now Hunter was puzzled. 'I don't understand why you waited nine years and are now so anxious to get to know your son.'

Adam grinned ruefully. 'Now I've met him, neither do I.' He walked over to the window and looked out, speaking over his shoulder. 'You see, I regretted my brief liaison with Susannah, didn't want to remember it. I was an only child so I had no nieces or nephews. It's reprehensible but I'm afraid I thought of children less as people than as pests. They were restless at concerts – or the excuse the members of the consort made if they had to miss a rehearsal. If I thought about him at all, I thought I'd never agree with Susannah about his upbringing and that he wouldn't thrive on the tensions between us. The older he grew, the more I thought I'd dislike the person he'd become under her influence. Half of his genes are hers and she'd have taught him all her opinions and attitudes.' He swung round and faced the two officers. 'He didn't learn them, though. As soon as I saw him yesterday afternoon I realized he was my son too. I didn't know what to do. He seemed happy. I wanted to get to know him but not to disrupt the life he was used to. I wondered if maybe Zannah had got married to someone rich. Luke obviously takes money and possessions for granted. Has she? Where is she?'

Hunter told him.

After a moment's shocked silence, a smile he repressed on his face appeared in his voice. 'Sergeant, could you tell me where I have to go to collect my son?'

Browne usually took upon himself the unpopular task of informing the next of kin of a victim's death. His team were happy to let him do it, assuaging their occasional pangs of conscience by agreeing that he was the best man for the job. For this one he was taking Mitchell along. It was time he learned to be tactful and sympathetic. Browne was half relieved and half vexed, therefore, to find, when Julie Wilson opened the door to them, that she had already heard about her sister's death.

'Sue's friend Wendy rang Kevin this morning and asked him to break it to me,' she told Browne as she led the two officers into her very warm living room. She offered them seats and relieved them of their coats, then indicated the older woman slumped in the armchair in front of the blank television screen. 'I've been expecting you. I'm afraid my mother will have to stay with us. There's no one else here at the moment and she can't be left.'

'Won't it upset her?'

Julie shook her head. 'She won't take it in or remember you were here. Kevin's taken the children out to give me some peace. What can I do?' Apparently quite composed, she settled herself so that she could both attend to them and observe her mother.

'Could you tell us about the last time you saw your sister?'

Julie described the trip to the hospital, her grip on herself becoming less certain. 'The doctor told Susan last night that the cancer is inoperable. Dad will only live a few more weeks. He wants to come home but I'm at full stretch already.' She scrubbed at the tears angrily. 'Sue said she'd come over today and we'd work something out between us. Now I'll have to deal with it all.'

There were sounds of new arrivals in the hall. The door was flung open and a young boy burst in, jostling his mother in his exuberance. 'We're back.' She rounded on him furiously. 'That hurt!' She held her arm where he had caught it and burst into tears. The boy's face registered astonishment rather than dismay. He was obviously used to greater tolerance. It was hardly surprising that his mother was overwrought. Browne wondered if it would be kinder to let her recover a little longer from her double blow. There were plenty of other leads to follow in the meantime.

She responded quickly, however, to her husband's practical sympathy in the form of a further removal of her sons and a promise of strong sweet tea. Mitchell completed the temporary cure with the matter-of-fact tone of the question Browne had not dared to ask. 'Were you close to your sister?'

She handed him back his handkerchief and sniffed. 'I suppose not. Not lately. It was a pity. We did everything together as kids but her going to university did for that. I never really felt I knew her after she came back. I suppose it stands to reason. Her whole outlook had changed.'

'But wasn't that the whole point of her going?' Mitchell said. 'To change her outlook, to enlarge her horizons.'

She looked surprised at this – from a policeman. Her husband brought in the tea, inspected her carefully, then nodded his agreement to the continuation of the interview. She took her cup and watched through the window as Kevin, who had gone outside, organized a ball game with their sons. Mitchell joined her there.

The game was becoming fast and furious, and satisfied that her husband had the children in hand she turned to Mitchell. 'Sue came home at the end of her first term in half a mind not to go back. She said it wasn't the place for people like us. I knew Mum and Dad would be dreadfully disappointed and I talked her round, told her she'd survive. She did it by becoming like them – got herself a posh new voice and a posh new name. Susannah!' She tutted. 'I think, in a way, Mum was glad when she got pregnant. She'd grown away from us and being landed with Luke brought her back to Cloughton. They were angry, though, when she wouldn't tell us who the father was.'

'Wouldn't tell . . .?'

Browne frowned fiercely at Mitchell, who became silent, whilst his CI brought Julie back to the table with a request for more tea. 'Did she say later who it was?'

She passed Browne's full cup and shook her head. 'No. We wondered how she'd manage. Kev and I had Lisa and Steven to provide for by then and the parents had nothing to spare. But Sue always fell on her feet. She found work she could do at home – she was qualified of course.'

Mrs Farrar, in the depths of her armchair, had been tugging at her woollen cardigan till she succeeded in removing it. Julie went over to her. 'Put it on, Mother. You'll get chilly and we can't do with the fire turned up even higher.'

The older woman bridled. 'That man had it on. I'm not going to wear it.'

Julie raised her eyes to the ceiling and sighed. 'All right. Steven will fetch you another one in a few minutes.' She turned to Browne apologetically. 'She's convinced a man broke into her room and put on her clothes. She refuses to wear anything he's supposed to have worn. It's funny that she can always remember things that she's imagined when she forgets everything that's really happened.'

Her brow wrinkled as another problem occurred to her. 'What about Luke? He can't stay with this Wendy woman for ever.' She began to run her fingers through her hair. 'I'm fond of the bairn. I suppose we could squeeze him in here, but...' She made a vague gesture that seemed to indicate all the difficulties this plan would involve, her cramped quarters, the contrast with what Luke was accustomed to, her preoccupation with her mother, and the boy's inability to tolerate his cousins' boisterous behaviour.

'I don't think there'll be any problem about money. Sue will have had insurances and so on. She was keen about things like that. In fact, that would be the chief difficulty. My three are already jealous of all Luke's possessions without having them thrust under their noses all the time. Anyway, they don't get on. Sue offered to take Steven to the hall with Luke yesterday but he wouldn't go – said he'd been out with them before and it was always boring. Not in front of Sue, thank goodness.'

'I'm sorry.' She shook her head. 'You're policemen not social workers. You don't want to hear all this.'

Browne put his cup on the table and reached for his coat. 'We aren't monsters. Of course you're preoccupied with practical problems. We can put you in touch with people who'll help you sort things out.'

Mrs Farrar was still shuffling restlessly in her corner, pleating and unpleating the hem of her dress. Looking up, she addressed Browne. 'Have you been looking for Peter? I don't know where he's gone. I never thought he'd leave me.' The old woman was dry-eyed but despairing.

Tears rolled down Julie's cheeks and Browne felt his own eyelids pricking. Julie went across to her. 'You'll see him again tomorrow, Mum.' She squeezed her mother's shoulder, then turned back to Browne and the subject of her sister. 'I shan't rest till you've found out who did it.

The only thing I can do for her now is to help you. But what . . .?'

'If and when there's something, we'll come again. We're anxious to know about the phone call that summoned her away. You've no theories about that?'

Julie shook her head and Browne buttoned his coat. As the two officers took their leave, the old woman's voice followed them. 'Have they gone to look for Peter?'

Chapter Nine

On Monday morning, before Browne's team assembled for their briefing, he received a phone call. The Smith family had heard the early morning news and thought he ought to know about the injured woman Vanessa had picked up on Saturday evening. Browne agreed that he needed to know all about it and the girl promised to come to the station there and then. Her voice, over the line, had sounded very self-assured, so when she appeared Browne was surprised to see that she was wearing the brown and cream uniform of a local comprehensive school. 'Miss Smith?'

She answered his unspoken comment. 'I'm nearly eighteen, been driving for almost six months. It's silly, isn't it? You can get married at sixteen but you can't drive a car till you're a year older or buy a drink for another year after that.'

She collapsed in a heap into the chair he indicated, the usual growing-teenager's method of sitting down. Mitchell came in. Browne waved him to another chair and indicated that he should make notes.

The girl beamed at him. 'My name's Smith, Vanessa Maria. Being saddled with the plainest and commonest of British surnames, my parents plumped for the fanciest first names they could think of.'

'Oh dear!'

Mitchell and Vanessa turned to Browne enquiringly.

'My surname's probably the second commonest and I

called my daughter Virginia Elizabeth. Now I know why.' They laughed. 'Would you repeat what you told me over the telephone whilst DC Mitchell writes it down?'

The girl gave a lucid account of picking up the injured woman and dropping her outside the hospital casualty department. 'I parked the car and gave Dad a quick ring. I had a job getting him to believe I wasn't just inventing a story because I was going to be late. He apologized to me this morning when I heard the news and wanted to talk to the police. Anyway, I'd been away a few minutes. When I came back to the waiting room I couldn't see the girl so I went to the nurse at the desk and said I was with her for the time being and I'd give her a lift home when they'd finished patching her up. They didn't know what I was talking about. The girl hadn't reported to them and she'd completely disappeared.'

She enjoyed the effect this revelation had on them before continuing. 'I suppose I can see why Dad thought it was a tall story.'

Browne produced the photograph of Susannah and Luke that had been found in her car. 'Can you tell me if this is the woman you picked up?'

She studied it carefully for several seconds, then shrugged. 'I only saw her by street lights. She was certainly very fair. She was wearing a loose coat so I'm not even sure of her build. It could be.'

Browne took his photograph back and regarded the girl, assessing her. 'Would you be prepared to take a look at the body? It might help you to be more sure.'

She paused, facing the ordeal in her imagination, then nodded. 'All right.'

She was being borne away by PC Caroline Webster when Hunter arrived apologetically. 'Sorry. Mornings aren't good at the moment and Fliss behaving like an excited puppy doesn't help.'

Mitchell grinned. 'What about Tim?'

Hunter shook his head. 'He's taking it as a personal

92

affront. You'd think we'd done it on purpose to embarrass him.' He added, as he sat down, 'To be fair, I don't think I'd have taken too kindly to a new sibling in my late teens. Who was the little maid from school?'

They explained and Hunter, glad to be distracted from his domestic affairs, gave his mind to the case. Browne went on to describe their preliminary interview with the victim's family and Hunter's eyebrows rose as he dealt with the question of Luke's father. He gave the salient points from his own interview the day before. 'Who do we believe then? Holroyd claims he's always paid full maintenance. Is this a large porky because he's taken a fancy to the boy?'

'You think he might not be his father?'

'Not necessarily. I meant maybe he's only claiming to have paid in order to have some rights in the child.'

Mitchell shook his head. 'It's too easy to disprove if it's not true. But what about the mother? Was she keeping quiet about Holroyd's money so that she'd get handouts from the rest of the family?'

Browne thought not. 'They'd hardly have deprived themselves to keep Luke and Susannah in such obvious luxury.'

'Well, to claim benefits from the state?'

'They'd check. Her lifestyle would disqualify her.'

Mitchell capitulated and Browne began to plan their morning. 'You'd better give Holroyd another going over, Jerry. I've confiscated a great sheaf of bank statements from Susannah's office and I've an appointment with her bank manager at eleven. That should clarify things a bit. We'll need to see the family again but we'll leave them in whatever peace is possible for the moment.'

'I didn't get the impression,' Mitchell observed, 'that Julie Wilson knew much about her sister's finances and if she did I don't think she'd tell us. There's a fair amount of family solidarity there in spite of the two daughters' different outlooks and circumstances. Susannah seems to have made herself useful with the old folk to a certain extent even though Julie had most of the responsibility. She was apparently going to do something about her father in the weeks before he dies. I'm sorry for the daughter, Lisa. Too much responsibility will probably fall on her now.'

'What's going to happen to Susannah's boy?' Mitchell demanded. 'I suppose the courts will try to arrange what's best for him but I'm blessed if I can think what it is. I can't see him settling down happily at his aunt's house. Even she admits her kids don't like him. And the Allen woman won't want full responsibility for him even though she knows and likes him.'

'He'll probably go to his father – if Mr Holroyd can prove that he is – in spite of their being strangers to each other. It's certainly Holroyd's intention to take him and there's a woman on the scene to do the maternal bit.' Browne was anxious for work to begin. 'It's not our responsibility, Jerry. Go and do your in-depth study of Holroyd. I'm off to see Miss Farrar's bank manager when I've read the rest of these reports. You, Benny, can see who the family doctor is and what he can tell us about the child and anything else that it seems good to ask him. We'll just have to hope that one of us comes up with something useful.'

With trepidation, Vanessa Smith followed PC Webster into the mortuary. All the surfaces were stainless steel, clean and shiny but a background sound of gurgling water reminded her that they had recently been cleared of unspeakable messes. She hoped her prim school skirt completely covered her shamefully trembling knees. Her hands were safely out of sight in her blazer pockets.

But when the sheet was drawn back from the dead woman's face she stopped shaking and examined it with interest, even though she knew from the radio news that a gaping neck wound would be revealed if the cover was

94

pulled a few inches lower. This was not a person any more.

PC Webster touched her arm. She had said to call her Caroline but Vanessa couldn't bring herself to do it. When she ignored the touch, the PC spoke. 'What do you think?'

She made up her mind. 'Not to swear to in court, mind, but . . . I think so.' As she was led out she began to cry.

PC Webster was concerned. 'She can't feel anything now. Come and have a cup of tea.'

Vanessa followed again, wiping angrily at her face. 'It wasn't seeing a dead body. It's just thinking that if I'd ignored that impatient driver behind me and taken her right in she'd be alive now.'

PC Webster wasn't so sure. 'This killer had two goes at her. When you got her away from him he tried again. It wasn't an impulse action in a crisis situation. He was determined to get back to her sometime.' Vanessa sipped her tea, uncomforted.

For Julie Wilson, her trip to Crossley Hall on Monday morning was almost a little holiday. Kevin was at work in his factory office, the boys and Lisa were at school and her mother temporarily but safely in the care of Mrs Pollard across the road.

Ruth Pollard had been on the borderline of neighbour and friend till today. Now Julie relegated her to being just a neighbour. She had agreed to 'mind' Mrs Farrar 'for an hour or so in the sad circumstances', a subtle intimation to Julie that she expected to be kept abreast of the circumstances and that her good nature was not to be taken advantage of when they became less sad.

Julie had averted her eyes as her bus passed the shelter that was still the centre of police activity, but now she was enjoying her walk through the grounds of the hall. She tried to work out how long it was since she had been out in the fresh air apart from her four-times-weekly scuttle to work through the dusk and back home through the breakfast rush. Her life seemed a twenty-four-hour round of mopping up after geriatrics, relieved only by more mopping up after her clumsy, boisterous sons.

Julie paused to regard the front of the hall, decided that it was pretty in an old-fashioned sort of way, and was glad as she climbed the steps to the entrance hall that she didn't have to chivvy Kevin into keeping the plaster cleanly white and picking out the elaborate black patterns with fresh paint.

She paused in the doorway to get her bearings. Beyond the reception desk a wide and spiralling staircase led to gloomy regions above, its rails and spindles elaborately carved to collect dust. The entrance hall itself was dim, the strength of the sun kept out by the greeny glass in the small leaded panes. What an age they would take to clean. She sympathized with her sons' reluctance to visit the place.

The chit of a girl at the desk looked startled to see her. Julie introduced herself. She learned in exchange that the girl was Miss Allen's assistant, Jane Griffin, and that Miss Allen and Luke were having tea and biscuits in the restaurant, busy discussing the problem of clean clothes for him. Julie felt comfortable again – this was the sort of problem she had come to deal with.

Before she could give voice to her offer the telephone on the desk between the two women rang shrilly. Julie gathered from Jane's end of the conversation that a pressman was trying to charm his way into the hall to take pictures of Luke and the room from which her sister had been called away. Jane Griffin, using Miss Allen's authority and that of the police, was firm in her refusal but polite, even chatty.

When she eventually replaced the receiver she smiled at Julie. 'I kept him talking as long as I could, listening to the background noise. I could hear that he was in a pub and that he had another reporter with him. He covered the mouthpiece to talk to him but I could hear his muffled insults about me and the police. There was a juke box playing – I think it was a Whitney Houston record.'

'What do you want to know all that for?'

She was anxious to explain. 'Because if I'd listened more carefully on Saturday night I'd have been more help to the police.'

'How?'

'Well, I might have had a clue where the person rang from.'

'I see – and you haven't?'

Jane shook her head mournfully, then cheered up again. 'The policeman said I could have heard something subconsciously and that it might come to the surface later. I'm to let him know if it does. It might pop up in the next day or two if I don't try too hard to remember. I felt really stupid. I couldn't even tell him if it was a woman or a man. By the way, I'm very sorry about your sister.'

She didn't sound sorry but Julie realized that the girl was more embarrassed than unfeeling. She was not sure herself how she felt about Sue's death, except very stressed and alone with her problems.

Suddenly the girl beamed. 'Do you know, I have remembered something!'

'What?'

She shook her head. 'I'd better not tell you. Sergeant Hunter told me not to discuss it.'

Julie shrugged. 'Please yourself. Did you say Luke and Miss Allen were in the coffee place?'

Anxious not to give further offence, the girl let her visitor pass behind the desk and take the short cut through the kitchen to the restaurant, though she could not hide her delight in having a clue to offer. 'I think I'll call at the station instead of ringing. I've never seen the inside of it.'

*

97

Luke was less than enthusiastic about his aunt's visit though his polite greeting became more sincere when he realized her arrival did not mean his imminent removal to her house. Experienced in handling adults, he wisely remained silent whilst the two women discussed Aunt Julie's cramped quarters and arranged the loan of Steven's shirts and underwear until the police were finished in his house and allowed him to collect his own. He listened approvingly as Wendy expressed her appreciation of his company and her willingness to keep him for the time being.

He noticed that his aunt too approved the arrangement. He understood that, in her way, she was quite fond of him although she had even less idea what went on in his head than his mother had had. He gave a gracious consent to their suggestion that he should return to school the next day.

'I'll collect the things,' Wendy was saying as he nibbled his third biscuit. 'Don't you drive over again.'

'I came by bus. I don't drive.'

Aunt Julie looked cross at having to make the admission and Wendy was embarrassed as she offered, 'We'll take you home and pick them up now. It should be Jane's coffee time but she'll have to have it at the desk. I'll let her go home at half four this afternoon in compensation.'

It would be good to be back at school, Luke decided. He would be able to discuss with Javed how a boy whose mother had been killed ought to behave. Even Wendy, who knew him quite well, seemed surprised that he wasn't crying. But then, neither was Aunt Julie, or Wendy or anybody. Perhaps they too felt rather relieved that she was no longer around.

Caroline Webster was invited to Browne's afternoon briefing to deliver her report in person. She repeated Vanessa's qualified assertion and accepted Browne's thanks. 'She wishes she'd seen the woman alive without

98

her coat on. I showed her the dead woman's shoes. She said she didn't look at them on Saturday but she had the impression the heels were the same height. What she is sure about is the time – because of getting the car back before her father's deadline. She saw the woman between ten to and five to ten and dropped her outside casualty at five minutes past . . .'

There was silence for consideration until Mitchell, as usual, was the one to break it. 'There are endless possibilities. The killer could have followed Smith's car to the hospital, got hold of the woman again, killed her in the hospital grounds and dumped her body in the bus shelter.'

Browne shook his head. 'Ledgard thinks she was killed where we found her.'

'If she'd had a bang on the head,' Hunter ventured, 'she might have wandered about the hospital grounds in a daze and been picked up again.'

'I've got people searching. If there's evidence for that, we'll find it.'

'Someone must have forced her.' Mitchell interrupted his father-in-law and senior officer without compunction. 'Otherwise, why would she go back to the area where she'd been attacked, even if she were capable of getting so far, which doesn't seem likely?'

Jennie Taylor spoke for the first time. 'Maybe that's where she'd been going originally. It might be where she lives.'

After another silence, Hunter volunteered, 'There's a coat somewhere, bloodstained, with a rent in the sleeve.'

This set up a new train of thought which they all followed. 'There was no coat in Susannah's car. Did she leave hers at the hall?'

'The jacket she was wearing was reasonable protection. The evening was cool but October's been much warmer than usual.'

'Would you have worn a coat over it Saturday night, Jennie?'

She considered, then shook her head. 'It didn't look remotely like rain. I think I'd have wanted to show that suit off rather than cover it up.'

Browne nodded. 'All right. Let's press on. I had quite a profitable session at the bank.' He displayed the statements he had found in Susannah's desk. 'I haven't gone into the payments made by various magazine publishing houses and so on, though we'll follow those up later if need be. What interested me were the four monthly cheques that I've marked, paid into her account by private individuals.'

'Blackmail, then?' Mitchell's inevitable interruption was preceded by a whistle. The team ignored him and continued to look at the CI.

'Benny has made the obvious suggestion,' he went on crushingly. 'You'll notice that the amounts vary. The smallest, you'll be interested to hear, is the gift of our friend Adam Holroyd, so his is child maintenance rather than protection money. We'd better try to find out what hold she might have had on the others. One's an Asian, living in Leicester – Singh by name so he'll very likely be a Sikh. Another is named Milton and lives in Sheffield and the enormous amount is from a chap called Hanson from York.'

'So the good news is that we can all go on our travels tomorrow.' They all glared at the irrepressible Mitchell, but then, with the exception of Jennie Taylor, looked pleased with the idea.

'Did you get anything out of the doctor, Benny?'

Mitchell grinned. 'As much as there was. It turned out to be our friendly police surgeon Stocks, so without any breach of his professional code, of course, he told me all – at least there was no self-important hemming and hawing. Susannah Farrar was in robust health and so is her frail-looking son. Completely trouble-free pregnancy but breech birth. He doesn't know who the father is. Old Mr Farrar is dying of cancer that could have been treated if he'd complained earlier. Unfortunately its onset coincided

100

with his wife's first symptoms of Alzheimer's disease. He was too busy looking after her to worry about himself. She'd wander out and get lost, cause scenes in local shops because she couldn't cope with money any more. Apparently there are three stages that progress to the full-blown disease over about ten years, but hers has developed more quickly and she's got into the second. She talks nonsense and puts her clothes on backwards and eats flowers, and so on. And she wanders about at night. The Wilson family do shifts watching her. They had enough on without a murder investigation.'

As the rest of the team nodded soberly, the telephone rang. Browne took a message and thanked his caller. 'That was the headmistress of Luke Farrar's school. Apparently an Asian man has been hanging about the playground asking about the boy. She was going to speak to his mother about it. When she heard the news about her she tried us instead.' He turned to Hunter. 'Any further revelations from Holroyd?'

Hunter shook his head. 'Not really. He knew the child's birth certificate didn't name him but he was prepared to pay up as soon as he knew Susannah was pregnant. Said he couldn't let the child suffer for their differences. He's not at all upset about her death, just excited at the prospect of having the boy.'

'That's not decided yet.'

'Try telling him – and we'll have to go to Bath now to ask him anything else. He took today off work but both he and the girl have jobs to go back to. He's gone to the hall to say a temporary goodbye to the boy. I've got addresses for him and for the girl, Karen Atkins. Right, Jennie, sum up.'

Jennie blinked. This appeal was usually made to Hunter. After several seconds' thought she made a succinct attempt. 'Someone phoned Susannah Farrar at Crossley Hall on Saturday night and she went out to meet him.'

'Or her.'

'All right. Later, Vanessa Smith picked up an injured girl on the road between the hall and town and took her to hospital. The girl wandered away, returned to the same area and was killed. Or, someone attacked two girls, one of them was walking-wounded and shocked, then the story as before. Either she's back home, or wandering around, still in shock, or the killer got back to her and there's a second body somewhere. Then, four people were paying cheques into Susannah's account. Holroyd claims his was child maintenance. Maybe it's true, or maybe Susannah was blackmailing him for some other reason. An Asian has been hanging around Luke Farrar's school. He may or may not be one of the four cheque-payers. We don't know why three of them are paying up.'

Browne nodded his satisfaction with this summary. 'Right, tomorrow we'd better go and ask them.'

Jane Griffin's day had been more entertaining than she had expected. Leaving her flat, reluctantly, that morning, she thought it hardly worth opening up the hall. No school party was booked in and the general public hardly rolled up in droves on Mondays.

She had reckoned without the events of Saturday night, though. She had left for home after the concert before anyone had become seriously worried about Susannah Farrar. She was well aware that that rat Craig Reynolds had sneaked off to the opening of the *Blue Dahlia* with someone else, rather than wait till her extra duty was over. No sweat. He wasn't the only fish in the sea. She'd decided to look up David Garston again, with consequences that had restored her self-esteem. The sort of Sunday she had spent with Dave at his place had not included watching the television news, so she'd no idea that the brief visit she'd had from that policeman had been part of a murder investigation. She had been surprised, this morning, to see the little boy still at the hall. She was not surprised at all, nor sorry either, to hear that

102

someone had done for that stuck-up Susannah.

She'd noticed that Wendy had been surprisingly on edge all day. Susannah was her friend, of course, but they weren't very close. She was better with the boy than his mother was, and Jane suspected she loved him more. It was Wendy who took him on repeated rounds of the hall, explaining everything, teaching him to value it. Jane even felt a bit of respect for the old things herself whilst she was listening to Wendy talking about them, though it soon wore off as she sat in the gloomy entrance hall by herself.

Where, she suddenly asked herself, had Wendy been when that mysterious phone call came? Not buzzing round as usual. And she'd disappeared again after Susannah left. The body had been found just down the road from here. And she'd almost adopted the child already.

The more she thought about it the fonder Jane grew of her theory that Wendy knew more than she was saying. Perhaps she shouldn't have told her she'd remembered about the phone call. Perhaps she'd have more information to offer to Sergeant Hunter than he'd bargained for.

It was hearing Whitney Houston in that phone call today that had made her remember the piano in the background on Saturday playing 'Lily of Laguna'. She knew that tune. Her granddad used to sing it to her gran. Suppose Wendy had nipped over to the pub across the road and made the call from there. There was often a live pianist at the Shepherd's Rest, playing the old songs. Jane glanced at her watch. Where was Wendy now? She'd said she'd take over the desk at four thirty so that she could leave early. It was four thirty-five now. She'd keep her appointment with Sergeant Hunter. If someone got into the hall without paying it would be Wendy's fault.

Jane got out her make-up mirror and fixed her face and hair. Wendy would be annoyed if she caught her 'prinking and preening' at the desk. Still, it had been Wendy's own suggestion that Jane have her coffee there this morning

103

and usually she went wild if she caught her eating or drinking when she was supposed to be on duty. Now, she was ready and she would go. Cheerio to all these stuffy old things until tomorrow. Leaving the desk unattended and the front door open, she went down the steps and across the flagstones.

Suddenly, a figure appeared, beckoning to her from the entrance to the Yew Tunnel. 'Can you help me? There's a girl collapsed in here and I think she's hurt.'

Jane hurried to assist. Three minutes later a girl really was collapsed in the tunnel. She really was hurt, fatally injured in fact. Her name was Jane Griffin.

Chapter Ten

When he set out for Leicester on Tuesday morning, Hunter left his wife in the capable hands of his twelve-year-old daughter. He grinned, remembering Annette's accusing glare at him as Fliss, beaming, tripped into the bedroom with tea and toast she could not face. It was early and he drove through traffic-free streets to pick up his CI. Browne was watching for him from his sitting-room window.

As he came out and settled himself in the passenger seat, Hunter clicked on the tape recorder and both men jumped as their ears were assaulted with Magnum fortissimo. With a grimace the sergeant ejected the tape, scrabbled in the pocket on the driver's door and pulled out some Vaughan Williams. 'We'll try "The Lark Ascending".' He grinned as his CI's expression indicated that for him this was only the lesser of two evils.

After a minute or two, Hunter disposed of this second choice of music. 'It's not a piece that marries well with the purr of a car engine.'

'What about the cacophony we started with? Are you trying to broaden your mind?'

Hunter shook his head. 'It was Tim's seventeenth birthday last weekend. I said if he could behave like seventeen instead of seven, I'd give him a driving lesson. He framed very well but apparently adolescents can only concentrate with a background of that kind of noise. Anyway, since then we haven't had any snide remarks about the libidos of the elderly or making it into the *Guinness Book of Records.*'

The two officers had beaten the rush-hour traffic to the M1 and enjoyed a remarkably smooth passage to the turn-off for Leicester. Browne, who hated being driven, concentrated hard on the scenery.

Their progress was much slower on the congested roads leading to the central police station and they groaned when the desk sergeant directed them out again to the district sub-station close to the Singhs' house. There they encountered Inspector Blay, loquacious and hospitable.

Over a second breakfast with excellent coffee he explained why they had been sent to him. 'Actually, I'm the Community Relations Officer but my area contains thousands of Pakistanis so that the work with Asian women has expanded to take up about eighty per cent of my time. Many Asian families still try to live their traditional way here but their children have to go to school and grow up wanting the same choices as their classmates. Then, at fifteen or sixteen, the girls are taken to Pakistan for a holiday and come back married. Out of British jurisdiction they have no one to turn to. The intelligent ones ask us for help before it happens and we get them to a safe place. Some run away of their own accord and then their parents come in demanding I find them. We pass messages for them and arrange supervised meetings.'

He read impatience on their faces. 'I'm telling you all this because I've come across your people before – but nearly ten years ago. Singh's wife, Shahnaz, came to see me because she thought her parents were arranging a marriage for her. She was suspicious when they promised her a holiday but they said it was to be in France and showed her the plane tickets. Without telling her, they'd also put their house into her name and put money into a bank account for her. They'd let her go out to work too when most of her well-to-do friends were kept at home

106

after they left school. She didn't realize that having work and owning property qualified her to come back to England, bringing her husband with her.'

Hunter swallowed the remains of his bacon sandwich and began to make notes.

'The plane she thought would take her to France landed in the Punjab. She managed to get a letter to us from there but there was nothing I could do whilst she was abroad. That was a good thing, as it happened. As soon as she was introduced to Singh, she fell in love with him and agreed to the wedding without any fuss.'

'Wasn't she angry at being tricked?'

He shrugged. 'Well, maybe, but she was happy with her lot. They have a nice little family now, but she occasionally brings other youngsters in with their problems.'

Browne looked pointedly at his watch and the obliging inspector scribbled an address copied from a file and explained how to get there. From clear instructions they found it with no difficulty, driving through a rough housing estate to its upper echelon of newish, sizeable houses. They were typical of the rich English middle class except for a preponderance of red and orange paintwork.

The door was opened to the two officers by a slight girl with enormous brown eyes and a great deal of straight black hair. She was dressed in an outfit that was obviously a school uniform, except for the filmy brown trousers beneath the grey pleated skirt that were tucked neatly into her white ankle socks.

Hoping she understood him, Browne enquired for her parents. She replied in the Queen's English and a clipped private school accent that she would fetch her mother, then ran down the hall, calling out in what to him was a sing-song gibberish. There was a reply from within, equally unintelligible to the two officers, before a slightly taller, adult version of the beautiful child came to speak with them.

'Please excuse Shain. She doesn't mean to be rude but

our rule is English outside and Punjabi in the home.' The mother too spoke perfect English.

Browne nodded his understanding of the child's dilemma, produced his warrant card and introduced himself and Hunter. 'You are Shahnaz Singh?' She nodded. 'We were hoping your husband could give us some information about some former friends.'

'Policemen?' She looked more puzzled than alarmed as she ushered them inside.

'We're from Cloughton,' Hunter volunteered. This obviously meant nothing to her. 'In Yorkshire, near Bradford,' he elaborated.

'Inspector Blay sent us,' Browne added reassuringly.

Immediately she was at her ease. Another stream of Punjabi escaped the child. Her mother regarded her sternly. 'If you can't remember to speak English to our visitors then you had better read in your room until I am ready.' The child departed meekly. 'She has been to visit the dentist and I must return her to school soon. She merely said that maybe you had come to finish your business here so that Urfan need not return to Yorkshire.'

'He's been there recently?'

'On Tuesday he did business in Bradford, and again at the weekend, but not, I think, with policemen.'

Browne shook his head. 'We haven't met your husband. The friends we wanted to ask about are Adam Holroyd, Jonathan Milton and Matthew Hanson.' He frowned at Hunter, who was looking surprised. 'Does he still see them, talk about them?'

She shook her head. 'Not to me, but if they work with computers, he doesn't talk about his work at home.'

'Then perhaps you can tell us where to find him.'

The wailing of a very small infant interrupted them. Hurriedly, she gave them directions, and they left. Hunter turned the car neatly in the rather narrow road and, as they negotiated the corner, Browne saw Mrs Singh loading a carrycot into an estate car.

108

'Do we not mention Susannah to Singh either?' Hunter asked briefly.

Browne considered. 'Not till he's told us all about the other three,' he decided.

'If he knows anything.'

Browne nodded and stared straight ahead.

Urfan Singh was easily located in a square wood-panelled office in the square concrete building that was his father-in-law's place of business. Here, only the carpet was red, and that a rich but subdued wine shade. He had agreed to see them immediately and rose to greet them as they entered. Browne could see why his young wife had capitulated so easily. Singh was beautiful, tall and straight, broad-shouldered and slim-hipped with a flawless coffee-brown skin. He came to shake hands, moving with the casual grace of those few lucky adolescents who escaped both gaucherie and puppyfat. He placed the two officers in armchairs, treating them neither condescend-ingly nor obsequiously and asked how he could help them.

Having been warned that there were things not to say, Hunter waited for Browne's lead. Browne smiled pleas-antly. 'We'd like to know all you can tell us about Matthew Hanson, Adam Holroyd and Jonathan Milton.'

Whatever he had been expecting, it was not this. His expression was at the same time puzzled and guarded. He answered after several seconds' silence. 'They were my friends, a good few years ago. My university friends. Adam and Matt were studying English and Dr Milton was a lecturer, a professor, actually.' When the two officers remained silent he smiled at them and supplied place and dates.

Browne thanked him and Hunter wrote them down. 'And the subject you studied?'

'Computer science.'

'So why did you become friendly with Hanson and Holroyd?' Singh shrugged. 'You met socially, perhaps, over common interests?' He nodded but declined to elab-orate. 'So what were they? Beer?'

He shook his head. 'I am Sikh.'

'So, sport perhaps?'

He nodded vigorously. 'Yes, cricket I am very fond of. I played for two years for my university and all of the three years for my college.' Hunter realized suddenly why Singh had appeared familiar to him. He looked like a younger Imran Khan.

'And did Holroyd and Hanson play too?'

Singh laughed. 'For Adam it was always music and with Matt his God and his cars took up too much time.'

'So you all had music and cars in common?'

Singh replied with exaggerated politeness, humouring them. 'I am not musical, I am not even interested in Asian music, and then I did not have a car. Now I have a beautiful Porsche but I leave the bonnet down and value it only as an efficient means of transport.'

'So why were they friends of yours?'

'Why should they not be? Are you suggesting that nice young English students do not choose friendship with a Paki?'

His English, though grammatical, had not achieved his wife's nice grasp of idiom.

Browne asked, curiously, 'How long have you lived in this country?' then realized that, in context, the question was offensive.

'Long enough,' the Sikh told him icily, 'to have learned to wear shoes and eat with a knife and fork.'

To apologize would make things worse. He began afresh. 'It's perfectly reasonable that you and they should have a common friendship and interest. I'm merely asking what it was.'

'Why?'

Browne sighed. 'I suppose, being of naturally enquiring minds, they saw you coming out of a lecture one day and said to themselves, "Here's an interesting young man from an alien culture, following an alien religion and an alien academic discipline. It would broaden our minds to commune with him." '

Singh glared belligerently. 'Why not?'

From behind Browne, Hunter's voice asked, 'Have you seen any of them since you left your college ten years ago?'

Having as yet no quarrel with Hunter, Singh replied in a slightly more friendly manner. 'As a matter of fact, no. I have worked very hard to pay back my father-in-law for his goodness to me and I have four young daughters to provide for. There has been little time for social activities. When I am free I wish to be with my family.'

Browne's next question reminded him he was under attack. 'You're a very handsome man, startlingly so. Did either Hanson or Holroyd find you attractive?'

Singh was now very angry. 'I do not have to hear this!' He banged his fist on the surface of his desk and rose to his feet, breathing heavily.

'Let's leave the question of grown men since you find it offensive. How long have you been interested in little boys?'

Singh drew a deep, steadying breath. 'I am *not* a homosexual. I am *not* a paedophile.'

'Well then,' Browne smiled at him. 'Just one little boy at Oakwood School in Cloughton?'

Singh's lips scarcely moved. 'Where is Cloughton?'

Browne's smile became sweeter. 'It's where you send your monthly cheque. And it's near enough to Bradford to have been included in your trips there in the last few days. It's where you asked little Javed Qreshi about his schoolfriend. Perhaps if we take you to see him again it will remind you.'

'Do you deny going to this school and asking a small Pakistani boy where you could find Luke Farrar?' Hunter asked in a matter-of-fact tone.

Singh licked his lips. 'It seems there would be very little point.'

'Why were you interested in him?'

The brown cheeks dimpled as he smiled sadly. 'I thought I had every right to be. I thought he was my son.'

'Mr Singh, this is Luke Farrar.' Browne held out a snapshot of the flaxen-haired, blue-eyed boy.

The smile disappeared and the brown face became a tight mask as Singh waved the photograph away. 'Yes, I know. The second time I asked, on Friday evening, the child was pointed out to me.'

'So, what made you think . . .?'

Singh sat silent for some twenty seconds, slowly shaking his head, before raising it and looking at the wall behind both officers. 'I wanted to believe it. More after each of the girls was born. I am Sikh, brought up to believe that all are equally worthy, but every father, even English, wishes for a son.'

'It was the boy's mother you all had in common, wasn't it?'

Singh looked surprised. Browne thought this was genuinely a new idea to him. 'I don't know who she was with when she was not with me.'

Browne sniffed. 'Probably it was someone with fair hair and blue eyes. I expect you're very angry with her.'

He shook his head and the dimples reappeared. 'Not now. I know how fortunate I am to have my wife and my daughters. Susannah tricked me and took money from me, but fortunately I have become rich and my family did not suffer. Perhaps later Shahnaz and I will have a son. I may not even prosecute Susannah. If I did my family would hear about it and that would hurt them. But on Friday, I could have killed her.'

'On Saturday,' Browne remarked, laconically, 'someone did.'

Oakwood was situated in Heath Royd, the other salubrious area of Cloughton besides Crossley Bridge. The school's reputation was such that OAKWOOD, in gilt, outlined in black on green in neat painted letters, was enough to identify it. The word 'school' was omitted.

Caroline Webster remembered a brief relationship she had had with one of its pupils. She could recall very little about what the two of them had done together and even less about how and why they had parted. What came back to her now, very clearly, was the glimpse into another, richer world she had had, beginning with a trip up the tree-lined school drive in Neville's father's car, lent for the occasion, on the way to a very sedate sixth-form disco.

She knew, therefore, that the main school drive led to the senior school building. The prep school for the eight-to twelve-year-olds could be reached by a narrower branch of the drive leading off on the left, but it was quicker to park on the road by the side entrance and walk from there.

She smiled to herself at what she saw. Rather a far cry from the tarmacked yard where she had spent her own school breaks and lunch times. An area of grass and trees stretched towards an adventure playground where tubular-metal climbing frames rose above a flooring of some rubber compound.

The senior school, she remembered, an adaptation of one of the larger of Cloughton's gracious old houses. The prep school, screened by trees and shrubs from the main building, did not have to be in keeping with it. It was frankly modern, single-storeyed, made from light-coloured stone and a great deal of glass.

The head mistress seemed somewhat taken aback at Caroline's appearance, though she was nevertheless hospitable: 'I can't really add to what I told the chief inspector on the telephone,' followed only after the offer of coffee and an armchair.

'Perhaps you can tell me a bit about Luke.'

She looked astonished. 'You surely don't think he had anything to do with this tragic business?'

'Of course not.' Caroline refused the coffee and sat down.

'Well, he's bright, quiet, polite and ...' She waved a

113

hand in the air, seeking the right word. 'Sort of watchful. I often wonder what he's thinking about. Oh, and he's very musical. It's a pity his mother wasn't.'

'Why do you say that?'

Again, she paused to consider. 'Partly because he ought really to have begun to learn what we, perhaps mistakenly, call a proper instrument, but more because she couldn't share his pride and delight when he played.' She drummed her fingers lightly on her desk as she tried to think of more ways to help. 'I could send for Javed Qreshi.'

Caroline was tempted but shook her head. 'I'd better not question him without having his mother here.'

'No, of course not.'

Caroline endured the inevitable conducted tour. She saw much to admire but heard little to throw light on their investigation. Returning to headquarters, she found Browne, Hunter and Mitchell all out and, wondering what she was expected to do next, decided to make up her mind over a cup of coffee in the canteen.

PC Michelle Jackson, beside whom she chose to sit to drink it, was familiar with the school and interested to hear about her visit. As she listened, she demolished a large squashy vanilla slice.

Enviously, viciously, Caroline ended her account, ' ... and may your teeth rot, your face break out in spots and your waistline expand by six inches!'

Michelle grinned amiably. 'I was up there about six months ago.'

'At Oakwood?'

Michelle nodded. 'They've got posh accents and posh uniforms but they're just as nasty as any other kids inside.'

'So what did they want you for?'

Michelle kept her waiting as she added two spoonfuls of sugar to her coffee. 'Just a police presence to frighten the kids.'

Caroline was very surprised. 'Oakwood kids? Whatever were they doing? Wait a minute.' She dashed over to the

114

counter, lifted the little glass screen by its chrome-plated handle and slid a cream horn on to her plate. Her conscience attacked her even as she was paying for it but she resolutely consumed it as she listened.

'It started when one of the parents accidentally threw away a sheet of stickers – you know, the sort of things that come out of cereal packets that kids collect and stick on cards. When her child missed them, he had hysterics and wouldn't go to school. The mother couldn't understand it and eventually calmed him down by buying another packet of whatever cereal it was.

'Later she complained to the head, said she could see these collections of bird and animal pictures and so on were quite educational but that the head was obviously using too much pressure if her child daren't arrive without them. The head said she knew nothing about it and the class teacher didn't either. They went back to the child, who eventually explained that he had to leave the stickers behind a pipe in the boys' cloakroom for someone to pick up or he'd get into trouble. He flatly refused to be any more explicit.

'The more they enquired, the more kids they found who'd been threatened. The little Farrar boy had been very upset by it. He'd been told to provide a full sheet each week or the word would be spread that his father wasn't dead but in prison. They all refused absolutely to identify the tormentor and were really afraid. The original parent took her child away from the school.

'The head didn't know what she wanted us to do, but what she certainly didn't want was publicity of that kind. I went up there to talk to all the kids. I explained what blackmail was and made sure they knew it's a criminal offence. Nasty. They start young, don't they?'

Chapter Eleven

DC Mitchell marvelled that there was as yet no sound from his two-year-old son's room, then checked over the breakfast tray he had just set. Clean cloth, two plates, cup and saucer, teapot, milk in a jug, brown bread and sunflower-oil margarine. He added jam, which his wife never ate, for the sake of its colour and considered a wine glass to hold a flower from the garden.

Over the top, he decided. Virginia would laugh. She'd probably laugh anyway. He picked up the tray, carried it carefully down the hall and entered the bedroom with a flourish. The bed was empty. Disconsolately, Mitchell edged himself and his tray into the hall again and elbowed open the door of his son's room.

'Watch out!' Virginia's timely warning prevented him from disenthroning his son. Behind the door, Declan rose from his potty with dignity and held it out to his father. Mitchell unburdened himself of the tray, received his son's offering with uneasily simulated admiration and pleasure and disposed of it.

When he returned, Virginia was sorting clothes for washing whilst Declan was helping himself to bread from the tray with one hand and lifting the tea cosy with the other.

'Another dry night. That teapot's hot. Don't touch it! I should get some bedding dry today. I was thinking, if I'm going to be tied to the house with another baby, I might as well go straight on and do an MA. I said, don't touch

116

it!' Virginia addressed the middle of the room and left her menfolk to sort out which of her remarks was meant for which one.

'I was going to bring you breakfast in bed,' Mitchell explained, superfluously, answering none of them.

'Why?'

'That's what Jerry does for Annette. He comes into work late.'

She paused to regard him quizzically. 'The infants must be due almost the same week, I suppose. Well, you can do the same for me if you get me into this condition when I'm in the menopause.'

'They aren't so old.'

'She's thirty-eight and he's forty-one. If you want to get up early and do something useful, why don't you put in an extra half-hour's studying for your sergeant's exams?'

Declan abandoned his bread and the teapot and trod on Virginia's egg, which had rolled on to the floor when he tilted the tray. Mitchell shrugged at his wife's howl of rage, caught and removed the teapot and went off to prepare for his trip to York.

Driving along the A64 he tried to envisage the horrors of mornings with two small children, then, with relief, transferred his thoughts to his forthcoming interview. It took place just over an hour later in a comfortable furnished room that might have been described as elegant, but for its pictures. Perhaps, Mitchell decided, 'pictures' was the wrong word. The walls were decorated with large prints, one of a garden, one of a flowery meadow, each with a black-lettered Bible text superimposed.

Hanson proved to be a clean-cut young man straight out of an old-fashioned American film. It came as a slight shock to Mitchell when he spoke with an English public school accent. He wore a dark suit, a white shirt and a dull blue tie, narrowly striped with maroon and a trace of white. Mitchell thought that his idea of getting changed would probably be to put on another dark suit, a fresh

117

white shirt and a maroon tie with a blue stripe.

If his business had failed he would have been able to earn a good living modelling for a toothpaste manufacturer. His teeth were probably only the usual size and number but they grabbed attention when he smiled and laughed. As the interview went on, he smiled and laughed a good deal. Mitchell, having read the texts on the wall, was not sure whether he was demonstrating his joy in the Lord or his pleasure that the money was obviously rolling in so well.

At a first glance, Hanson had seemed to be in his early twenties, but the second told Mitchell about the sun lamp, and the blow dryer that had given fullness to the slightly thinning hair on the crown of the well-shaped head.

Hanson was at home on a Tuesday morning, he explained, because he was entertaining a client for lunch. 'A restaurant is more conventional but my housekeeper could teach most chefs a thing or two and a home setting is part of the company's ethos.'

'What does the firm make?'

Hanson shook his head. 'It doesn't. We're in advertising.'

'And your part in it all?'

Mitchell's antagonism towards the man thawed slightly when he smiled ruefully. 'Good question. My father's in his mid-sixties now but he's still pretty much in charge of organizing things. He certainly still holds the purse strings. He isn't the ideas man, though. We employ a whole team of those. I've never been quite sure exactly what my role is, other than boss's son. I'm no organizer and I don't have ideas. Grace, my sister, is the one with all the brains.

'There's one thing I do well, though. I project exactly the required image. All the producers of wholesome, honest products – and my father deals, knowingly at least, with no other – feel confident that they'll be wholesomely and honestly advertised when they meet me. I'm the front man.

118

'When Father retires, I shall double the salary of the MD and expect him to take Father's place.' Mitchell's prejudices had both melted and evaporated at this disarming self-appraisal. 'Did you say, when you rang, that you wanted to ask me about Adam Holroyd? I haven't seen him in years. I believe he's still living down in the Devon–Avon area.'

'It's the time when you did know him that I'm interested in.'

The exemplary housekeeper had spared time from her lunch preparations to bring in coffee. Whilst he poured it, Hanson collected his thoughts and Mitchell, as he tasted it, wondered if he could wangle an invitation to lunch.

'We were all students together. Adam was one of the crowd that I spent time with when he wasn't organizing an ancient music practice and I wasn't at a Bible study.'

Mitchell felt that there was a lack of the fervour the texts had led him to expect. 'You make your religious activities sound like a hobby, on a level with the music.'

Hanson laughed. 'They weren't on a level at all. Adam genuinely needed and believed in his music. My enthusiasm was all sham.'

'But why?'

Hanson answered by merely stating, 'Those texts on the wall were a housewarming gift from my father.'

Mitchell nodded. 'I see. So what more can you tell me about Mr Holroyd?'

Hanson shrugged. 'What sort of information do you want? He liked a drink. He was bright – we were all a bit surprised when he only got a two-two. He hadn't, still hasn't I suppose, any brothers or sisters. No parents either. I'm not sure what happened to them but he was brought up by his grandparents and they both died, one in his first year at college and the other one just after finals. He was too upset on degree day to stay for the junketings.

'It's all coming back to me. Stop me rabbiting on when

119

you've got enough.' He stopped, suddenly. 'Here, I'm not dropping him in it, am I? He was such a pleasant, cheerful bloke that it never occurred to me that the law might have something against him.'

Mitchell ignored the question and asked, 'What about girlfriends?'

Hanson's brow wrinkled as he searched his memory. 'He gave one or two girls a whirl, usually musical ones. Nothing serious that I know of.'

'Was one of them Susannah Farrar?' Hanson shook his head. 'We have reason to believe that he had a close liaison with her.'

'*Adam?*'

Mitchell watched Hanson closely. The news had obviously shaken him. 'Is there anything wrong with that?'

Hanson rallied. 'Of course not. I just didn't know about it.'

'What about Urfan Singh?'

'Susannah used to flirt with him. He was very good looking. He wasn't really in our crowd.'

'Who was Jonathan Milton?'

Hanson blinked. 'He wasn't a student. He was my long-suffering tutor and professor. We didn't exactly get on. He thought I was a rich layabout who'd come to university for the wrong reasons. He was right but I didn't appreciate him saying it so often or so publicly.'

Mitchell hopefully handed his cup back and accepted a refill. He drank half of it before quietly resuming his questions. 'Did you know that Susannah was pregnant when she left college?'

Hanson sat still and silent for several seconds, then relaxed and nodded. 'Yes, I believe I heard that though I didn't know at the time.'

Mitchell got up and reached for his coat. 'Thanks for your time. That's about all then, except to give you the sad news that Miss Farrar died on Saturday.' There was a long silence. Hanson did not interrupt it with expressions of regret. It was impossible for Mitchell to decide whether the silence was sad, shocked, or merely wary. 'Oh, by the way, have you seen or heard from any of the people we've talked about since you all went your separate ways?'

He watched Hanson's inward debate and was not surprised when he shook his head. 'Not that I remember.'

It was clear to Mitchell that, whatever Hanson had rejected of his father's beliefs, he was not comfortable with lies. Let him worry about it over his five-star lunch. He would plan his own afternoon over a more modest one.

He had parked his car to one side of the circular lawn, round which the old carriage sweep made reversing unnecessary. Completing the circle and meeting the drive down to the road meant passing the window of the drawing room where he had so recently been sitting. Through that window, huge and un-netted, Hanson could be seen with a telephone receiver in his hand.

Mitchell took his car sufficiently far down the drive to be out of sight from the house. He climbed out, shutting the door silently and made his way on foot to the front door again. When Hanson answered his ring, he apologized profusely. 'Almost forgot. The CI was most insistent that I ask if you could lend us any photographs of the friends we've been talking about – photographs from that period.' He prayed that they would be upstairs and apparently they were.

Swiftly, as his heels disappeared above eye level, Mitchell re-entered the drawing room and located the mobile phone he had seen in Hanson's hand, now dropped carelessly on to a chair. He pressed the redial button and a pleasant light baritone voice sounded. 'Jonathan Milton. Can I help you?'

Hunter was pleased that Browne was ready to leave Leicester before the early evening rush-hour traffic had begun to build up. With luck, he could nip into headquarters, clear his desk and be home in time to get the family meal ready whilst Annette put her feet up. His desk proved to be miraculously empty of those dreaded little notes and messages and it was barely four thirty as he slid a little guiltily past Bennett's desk in the foyer.

He rejoiced too soon, however. Before he reached the swing doors, PS Bennett's voice called him back. 'You're wanted up in your CI's office, Jerry. There's another corpse waiting for you.'

Hunter's face fell and he turned wearily towards the lift rather than the stairs. 'Do me a favour and ring Annette for me, would you? Tell her I'll be late.'

Bennett nodded amiably and began to dial. Hearing the engaged signal, he replaced the receiver. Five minutes later he tried again. Still engaged.

Annette Hunter sighed. 'He monitors every breath I draw, lets me know where he is twenty-four hours a day and wants a progress report every minute. I don't think I can stand nearly another seven months of it. I wish I hadn't told him yet. Oh well, I suppose I'd better get some housework done. If I haven't completed the usual round he'll assume it's because of an imminent miscarriage plus nervous prostration. Be in touch?'

Virginia Mitchell replaced the receiver at her end and grinned to herself. So Annette wanted her to know how attentive her husband was. She'd be surprised if she knew how nearly Benny was rivalling him. She hoped that Annette would make the next call briefer. Now she wouldn't be able to finish her book before Declan woke up.

Hunter put his head round Browne's door. 'Who now?' He lifted a straight chair from against the wall, placed it with its back to Browne's desk and sat down, propping his chin on the back.

'Jane Griffin, the young assistant at Crossley Hall. Found in the grounds just after lunch today, strangled.

122

Happened late yesterday afternoon apparently.'

'So why did it take nearly twenty-four hours to find her? Didn't her folk panic straight away, knowing she had a slight connection with another woman's death?'

Browne shrugged. 'Apparently not. She was allowed home early because she'd given up her coffee break in the morning. It seems she was on her way to see you.'

Hunter sighed. 'She'd remembered something about that phone call?'

'I don't know. Very possibly. It's the usual story. She shares a house with several other girls. They each have a room and don't spy on each other. If she's missing at night, they assume she's with her boyfriend. She should have seen him last night but she'd let him down before, so he was irritated, rather than worried, when she didn't show up.

'Her mother rang the house several times. She'd taken to doing that since the body was found on Sunday and the girls, including Jane, were half amused, half impatient about it. When there was still no answer from her daughter after eleven, the mother broke her own rule and rang the boy's flat. The two of them waited up all night and finally rang us about half past four this morning. We couldn't do much till it was light but Bennett called Wendy Allen. She rang back about nine to say Jane hadn't shown up.'

'The hall's shut on Tuesdays,' Hunter volunteered.

'So we were informed, but the two of them go in as usual. There's always tidying to do, minor repairs, accounts to keep up to date. She said Jane wasn't too fussy about her timekeeping on Tuesdays, but by then we felt justified in taking the dogs in.'

'So why did it take till after lunch?'

'Because there were Jane-tracks everywhere. Dozens of tracks just led back to the house or out of the gate to the bus stop. Eventually, they found her under some sacking in what's called the Yew Tunnel.'

Hunter was sorry about that. It would never be quite

the same walking through it in future. Bennett had apparently tracked down Mitchell, who now tapped on the door, collapsed into Browne's armchair and listened to a repetition of his story whilst Hunter made notes on the points that interested him. 'You were soon on top of all that information,' he observed.

Browne smirked, but then displayed the neatly typed sheets inside the folder on his desk. 'Jennie was around. She typed it all up for us before she went. She's coming back in if she can sort something out for Lucy.'

On cue, Jennie appeared and accepted the armchair that Mitchell vacated for her. 'The Lord bless all mothers-in-law.' She turned to Browne. 'Dr Ledgard came in just before you arrived. He was muttering "petechial haemorrhages" and "vitreous humour K" and "cyanosis" as though they were swear words. He said rigor had been fully established and there was even a slight slackening in the face and jaw muscles. He said we could reckon on twenty hours, very roughly.'

She shuddered slightly as she recollected her second corpse of the week. 'Even I could see that she'd been strangled. There were the marks round her neck, of course, and dried blood and froth on her mouth and her nose had bled. Anyway, he's ringing you later this evening.'

'So, whoever killed her got busy as soon as she put her nose out of the hall – might even have known she would be leaving early and been waiting for her.' Mitchell wandered round Browne's office in search of another seat then propped himself against the windowsill.

'Our customers now need an alibi for yesterday teatime as well as Saturday night.'

Browne looked sharply at Hunter. 'You're quite happy that the same person killed both girls?'

Hunter considered. 'Not absolutely convinced, but it seems a reasonable assumption. If I'm right, does it let off any of the men we've seen today?'

Mitchell did a quick calculation. 'Hanson could drive here from York in about an hour, Singh from Leicester in two. It would take Holroyd about five hours from Bath. Still, we don't know he's there. We only know he said he was going.'

Hunter frowned. 'We're not after Holroyd, are we? Not for Susannah, anyway. He was in full view of his whole audience when she left the hall and he had Miss Allen and the boy with him on and off for ages afterwards, as well as that girl, Karen Atkins.'

'But, if they're in league, having an alibi for one killing isn't enough.'

'If who's in league?' Browne sighed. 'Start at the beginning, Benny.'

Mitchell happily described his day, making much of the fact that Milton's voice answered him on Hanson's telephone. 'Hanson's alibi for Saturday is his sister, but they've always got on well and are twins so we'll have to double check what she says. He claims they were both having dinner with their parents to celebrate their thirty-second wedding anniversary. Hanson looked very surprised when I told him that Susannah was dead.'

'So did Singh,' Hunter added.

'And so, doubtless, will Milton when we see him tomorrow,' Browne finished, grimly. 'I don't think that lets anyone off.'

The two senior officers gave Mitchell and Jennie the gist of their session with Urfan Singh. 'He gave us copious details of the nature of his business in Bradford. Jerry wrote it all down but I doubt if he understood any more of it than I did. We'll check the times of his meetings, but even if what he's given us is accurate, it doesn't account for the evening. Being Sikh and the socializing consisting mostly of heavy drinking, he went to his hotel room and did all his paperwork – so he says.'

'He was paying Susannah less than Hanson was,' Hunter put in, 'but it made a substantial hole in his income, especially in the early days, and he was desperate for his wife not to know.'

Mitchell fidgeted his ample rear on the narrow window-sill. 'He'd be even more anxious about his father-in-law finding out. The old man might possibly have turned a blind eye to a Pakistani affair, but Singh would be cut off without a shilling for messing about with a white girl.'

Jennie sniffed. 'If you ask me, Susannah Farrar got no more than she deserved.'

Mitchell grinned. 'Oh, I don't know. Such initiative! It's called recouping your losses. Are we assuming she was collecting from Milton too, on the same pretext?'

Browne shrugged. 'Someone will have to ask him tomorrow.' His telephone rang. He lifted the receiver, listened, then gave brief thanks. 'Ledgard,' he informed his team. 'He suggests that the strangling was done with something like a nylon stocking. The girl struggled. There are scratch marks on her neck where she scrabbled at the knot of the ligature.'

Jennie sat forward in her armchair. 'How long could it take? It was still broad daylight if we've got the timing right and the hall was still open. The killer was taking a big risk. And who'd want to kill this girl?'

'You typed the report. It says she was on her way to see Jerry.'

'Oh, yes. What about?'

They all looked at Hunter, who shook his head. 'I don't know. She never got to me, did she? I did tell her to think hard about that phone call on Saturday and to let me know if anything else came back to her, sounds in the background and so on. If we're lucky, she'll have said something about it to Wendy Allen.'

'In that case,' Mitchell warned, darkly, 'we'd better keep a close eye on Miss Allen too.'

Hunter broke the glum silence that descended. 'So what now?'

'I'm open to suggestions.'

126

They came thick and fast and Browne held up his hand to quell the babble. 'Jennie?'

'I think we should pump the sister – Susannah's, I mean for some inside information.'

Seeing that Hunter had begun one of his customary prowls round the office, Mitchell left his uncomfortable perch on the windowsill and appropriated the vacant chair before voicing his objection. 'I don't think she's got any. If Susannah confided in anyone at all, she'd choose someone with similar values and outlook. She only talked to Julie about family matters, gave a hand with the parents, asked her to mind Luke now and then.'

Hunter glared as he saw he had been deprived of his chair. 'Who did you have in mind?'

Mitchell ignored the glare and answered the question. 'Wendy Allen. If Susannah and Wendy spent as little time together as Wendy makes out, then it's odd that she's taken the boy over and that he's so happy to stay there with her rather than his aunt. I think we should talk to her again – and to the boy himself.'

Browne nodded. 'You've got yourself a job for tomorrow, then, but be careful with the boy. Jennie, you go with him. Find out between you about both victims' current men friends and show the photographs to Miss Allen and the boy.'

'What photographs?'

'Of the four sleeping partners, of course – which they are in every sense. In the meantime, we've got a whole army of people on house to house and so on in connection with both deaths. We'll just have to hope it throws something up. We all need food now, but at eight o'clock I shall be in the Fleece, in the course of my duties, naturally, to see what light alcohol can shed on the case. Anyone with a similar dedication to their work will be welcome to join me.'

Chapter Twelve

On Wednesday morning, Mitchell reverted to his more usual morning routine. He rolled over in bed, ignoring the noises of his son entertaining himself, even the reverberating crash that had Virginia leaping out of bed. He rose at six fifty-five when the alarm dictated, padded down the hall to the kitchen, filled and switched on the kettle and warmed the pot.

Then he abandoned domestic duties and concentrated on the preparation of his person to face the day ahead. He had a careful routine for this. He was not vain, just meticulous and methodical. He followed, from habit now, the rapid fixed sequence that had enabled him to preserve the standards of cleanliness and neatness that were important to him whilst being raised as one of six children in a five-roomed terraced house.

Six minutes exactly were sufficient in the bathroom. He was about to leave it in search of the day's clean garments when he was unceremoniously pushed aside and his wife took possession. Guiltily he listened to her retching, and silently demanded of the world in general how an expectant father was supposed to know what his wife required on any particular morning.

He discovered that Declan was fully dressed and supposed that the potty routine was completed. He tied a bib round his son's neck, scooped him up into his high chair and left him to spoon his cereal alternately into his mouth and on to his plastic tray. Then he tried to decide what further assistance his wretched wife would find supportable.

Experience had proved that a sympathetic enquiry into her sufferings was out. He checked his son's room for revolting offerings but the potty sat behind the door, shiny clean, and the bed proved to be rumpled but dry. Perhaps he should ring Hannah and ask if she could take Declan for the morning. He would have been keener on this plan if his wife's mother were not also his chief inspector's wife. He sniffed. Surely, he couldn't smell bacon?

He returned to the kitchen to find Virginia removing two thick rashers from the grill. As she turned he saw that at least half the colour had returned to her face and grinned at her. Taking his share of the bacon, he pushed it between two thick slices of bread and watched thankfully as his wife began to dispose of her own with a reasonable show of enthusiasm.

Since he wasn't allowed to ask how she felt, he offered to wash up. When his offer was refused, he knew that the worst of the affliction was over for the day. He kissed his wife and son, removed second-hand cereal from his chin with his crumpled napkin, and departed, whistling, to the garage.

As he drove the short distance to Jennie's house, Mitchell reflected on the team's session in the Fleece the previous evening. Jerry had shamed him by turning up promptly. Mitchell himself had remained at home till Declan was safely asleep, partly to help Virginia but chiefly because the child's bedtime routine was one of life's pleasures. Still, Annette could put her feet up without any help from Jerry, and Fliss was only too pleased to be left to fuss over her. It was remarkable to him how Jerry had mellowed over the last two or three years. He no longer had apoplexy if a joke wasn't squeaky-clean, and his alcohol consumption had risen until it was almost healthy.

Jennie had not turned up at all. Mitchell had seen that

this worried Browne. He was beginning to realize himself that it was difficult to do CID work part-time. Jennie's attempts to do so had set a precedent in their Cloughton station and it was not working. Jennie was a good copper but only when her mind was one hundred per cent on the job and now it seldom was.

The three officers had given the case a thorough airing but alcohol had not had the beneficial effect on it that Browne had hoped for. The four men, the 'sleeping partners', had been duped because they were all living a pretence that they could not afford to have exposed: Hanson to be a devout Baptist, Milton to be the upright academic husband of an aspiring politician, Singh to be a Sikh who followed implicitly the example of his guru. Not Adam Holroyd, though. They had considered whether Holroyd could in any way have contrived Susannah's death. It would have brought him most of the things he asked of life, his son and the chance to dispose of his income as he chose, but they could not get away from the fact that the call came whilst his concert was in progress.

And now they had a whole lot more alibis to collect, for Monday afternoon. There had been a long discussion about the voice that made the phone call – high for a man, low for a woman. Holroyd's voice was light and fairly high-pitched. Singh's was lower but the slight sing-song of his accent suggested the more pronounced rise and fall of a woman's voice.

Mitchell had his own ideas about it. He had not yet met Miss Allen but he was becoming increasingly interested in her. It was odd that she seemed to have taken over Susannah's son. And, surely, a nylon stocking was a woman's weapon. And strangling would have been a nice clean way of getting rid of Jane Griffin if she had to take her place at the desk immediately afterwards. It would have been easy for her to find out what the piece of information was that the girl had been anxious to impart to Hunter. And if that information incriminated her, it would be easy for her to make up something else and send the police on a wild goose chase. Mightn't she be a frustrated would-be-mother, wishing for a son as much as Adam Holroyd did?

Mitchell drew up at Jennie's door and she scrambled into the passenger seat beside him. 'Are we going to the Allen house?' she asked.

Mitchell thought not. 'If we go to the hall, she won't be distracted by fears of being late opening up.'

Miss Allen and the two officers arrived in the gravelled car park simultaneously and Mitchell was surprised to see Luke climb out of the passenger seat of the other car.

'He wasn't well this morning,' Miss Allen explained, answering the raised eyebrows. She lowered her voice. 'It might be delayed reaction to his mother's death or it may have something to do with Wednesday being games day.' Then, louder, 'There's plenty he can do to help me if he feels better later on. What can I do to help you two?'

Mitchell jerked his head at Luke. 'These ladies are having some women's talk. Shall we men have a look at the hall?' He strolled past the foot of the great staircase and through the doorway to the main room where the concert had taken place.

The boy followed obediently. Reaching the Great Hall, he began a conscientious attempt to entertain Mitchell. 'Did you know that the slates on this roof weigh a hundred kilos each? And they're only held up on wooden pegs. That's the weight of three people in our class put together. Do you weigh a hundred kilos?'

Mitchell, who almost did, hastily changed the subject. 'Would you like to see some photographs?' As the boy took the first one, Mitchell's conscience smote him. Interviewing a nine-year-old child with no guardian present, and no other officer, was well outside his brief. Still, he comforted himself, most of his commendations had come from an initial ignoring of protocol.

'I suppose that's the man who came looking for me at

school,' Luke remarked, handing back the snapshot of Singh. Mitchell was startled. He would have to watch himself with this child. He handed over the next picture and the boy's eyes lit up. 'That's Mr Holroyd. I like him. He looks like a camel.'

Mitchell grinned. That was exactly what Hunter had said. Hunter, he imagined, would have been just such a child as this. He looked at the picture again but was not sufficiently familiar with camels to judge whether the comparison was fair.

There was no response from Luke when Mitchell handed him the two photographs Hanson had produced of himself and Milton, taken during his college days. 'Have you got any photographs of your family?' Luke asked him. Mitchell felt in his wallet and took out a postcard-sized print of Virginia and Declan. Luke studied it for some moments before remarking, 'Mrs Mitchell looks like a friendly cat and your little boy looks like a monkey, a nice baby one.'

Mitchell shared this opinion of his son's appearance but gave consideration to the new idea of Virginia as a cat. He could see what the boy meant but the cat, too, would have to be a nice one. 'Do you compare all people with animals?'

Luke's brow wrinkled as he considered the question. 'Yes, I suppose I do.'

'What about Miss Allen?'

They shared a mischievous grin before Luke decided, 'I'd better not tell you.'

'She thinks you've skived off school today because it's games.'

Luke shook his head. 'Not really. My mother told me it was important to be as good at games as you can even if you don't like them. So I tried more and then I didn't hate it so much.'

'But you weren't really ill this morning, were you?' The boy shook his head. 'So why did you want to miss school?'

'I like it really, but . . .'

'Go on.'

'Well, it's embarrassing at the moment, because every-one's treating me differently. They talk to me as if I'm only in year three, as if having my mother dead makes me younger. Mrs Dent called me darling yesterday and it nearly made me cry, but not because of my mother. That's something you don't want teachers to call you. I was frightened she might put her arm round me. I don't like people doing that.'

'Not anybody?'

'Well, maybe Gran, but nobody else. I wish Granddad wasn't dying. I'd like to live with him and Gran now, but I know I can't.'

'So what do you think will happen?'

The child shrugged his slim shoulders. 'Wendy said I'd be able to choose but I can't work it out. She said to think of the times when I've been really happy and that would help me decide.' Mitchell's grudging respect for the elephantine Miss Allen increased. 'I was happy on Saturday, listening to the music group and then playing for Mr Holroyd, but I couldn't go and stay with them. I wouldn't mind living with Javed. Everything's weird at his house but it's interesting and his mother's nice.'

'What about Aunt Julie?'

'She's nice and Uncle Kevin but the others aren't. We went there again yesterday and looked after Gran whilst Aunt Julie went to see the doctor. Gran's not sensible any more. I don't know if I'd be sensible if I lived with Steven and Wayne. At least Wendy didn't send me upstairs to play with them. Do you know, they haven't got any books, only a few comic-strip ones.'

Michell's conscience was gaining ascendancy and for the present he asked no more. 'Fancy kicking a ball around? I've got one in the car.'

'No, thanks.'

'What do you want to do then?'

Luke's face lit up. 'I could play you the piece Mr Holroyd gave me on Saturday.' He was already scrabbling in his satchel for his recorder. Mitchell thanked him gravely and sat down to listen. Sometimes he could hardly believe the things he found himself doing in this job.

Jennie Taylor knew she was being inconsistent, paranoid even. Yesterday she had been furious at being sent off to the house to study Susannah Farrar's personal effects 'from a woman's point of view'. She was missing out on Lucy's babyhood, squabbling with Paul, just so that she could be around to re-check what the men had had first go at, work too boring for them. Now, she was equally angry because Mitchell had been given the chance to chat to the child, and yet talking to children was usually regarded as women's work. She nodded towards the door through which Luke had disappeared with Mitchell. 'He's still with you then?'

Since this needed no reply, Miss Allen offered none. Jennie began again, more graciously. 'It does seem rather an imposition, the family leaving him with you.'

The curator smiled and shook her head. 'It's his choice rather than theirs. And he's company for me, and certainly no trouble. Zannah never allowed him to be.'

Jennie remarked, conversationally, 'He was quite an investment, wasn't he?'

Miss Allen asked, 'What do you mean?', but Jennie could see that it was without much hope that Susannah's duplicity could be concealed any longer.

'If you want us to find out who killed her, it would help if you told us what you know. Why didn't you?'

'*Nil nisi bonum* and all that.'

'So tell me now. DC Mitchell will keep Luke out of the way for a while.'

Since her revelation was inevitable, Miss Allen was evidently set on showing Susannah in the best possible light. She pulled out chairs behind the desk for both of them. 'She was determined, from her first knowledge of her pregnancy, that her baby should have nothing but the best. She told her family about it early on. They were very supportive but could do little for her financially and said the child's father must pay his share. Zannah couldn't bring herself to tell them that she didn't know which of her various men friends was responsible. As she thought about it, she came to the conclusion that anyone who might possibly have been the father, who had taken that risk – and his pleasure – should have some responsibility for Luke.'

'So she picked some out. Why those four?'

Not denying that there could have been others, Miss Allen enumerated the reasons. 'They were widely scattered about the country and hadn't much in common, so they were not likely to find out about each other. They all had pressing reasons to hush up any scandal and they could all afford to pay.'

'Even Adam Holroyd?'

Miss Allen smiled. 'I think he was the only one Zannah felt slightly guilty about. I must say, when I talked to him on Saturday, he seemed too pleasant a man to be treated like that. But I've been thinking meantime that, maybe, it's all right. Luke resembles Mr Holroyd a little and he's certainly very musical. Zannah wasn't, although she went to concerts sometimes because music was part of the big C.'

Jennie raised her eyebrows enquiringly.

'Culture. Maybe the others were paying for past pleasures and Adam Holroyd really was supporting his son. Anyway, they all paid up with very few objections, and between them they tripled the amount that Zannah earned. She really did spend most of it on the boy, and she'd put a lot by for when he's older and more expensive, you know, music lessons, sports gear, travel abroad.'

'A splendid house in the most prestigious area in Cloughton? Gucci suits?'

135

'She wanted to provide him with the right kind of background.'

The excuse sounded lame to both of them. Jennie could hardly believe that the reckless plan had succeeded for nine whole years. 'She must have panicked when the CSA was set up.'

Miss Allen shrugged. 'She did rather, once she found they interfered even with mothers who didn't ask them to. She thought she might get rid of them all, in an emergency, by saying she was marrying someone who intended to adopt Luke.'

'She seems to have been remarkably frank with you. Were you a fellow student too?'

'No, we go further back than that. We were at school together, Julie too. We lost touch when Zannah went off to college and for a few years after she came back. I couldn't reconcile dyed-blonde, smart-as-paint Zannah with mousy-fair little Susan who'd written my English essays in exchange for my doing her maths.' So, Susannah had had an eye to the main chance from her early days!

'Her worries were getting quite complicated, actually. Any of the men might have wanted a meeting with the boy when he was older and she had to think of a convincing tale to tell Luke. He was beginning to ask some questions about his father. Soon he'd be wanting to see his birth certificate.'

Jennie shook her head in disbelief. 'Didn't she think of all this before she started?'

Miss Allen shook hers in perfect understanding of her friend. 'For Zannah, no argument was strong enough if it prevented her doing what she wanted to do. She was wondering how she'd explain to everyone, when Luke was too old to qualify for maintenance, why the money had stopped pouring in. That's why she refused . . .' She stopped speaking as snatches of a lilting dance tune floated through from the Great Hall. They listened for a few moments before Miss Allen laughed. 'He's been practising that piece continually ever since the concert.'

136

There was a short break in the performance, then the instrument sounded again, a laborious rendering of the five or six repeated notes of 'Twinkle, Twinkle, Little Star'. Miss Allen looked puzzled.

Jennie had a mental vision that caused a bubble of laughter to rise. 'I think my colleague may be contributing an item to the recital.' Then, whilst Miss Allen was still off guard, sharing the joke, 'Tell me about Jane Griffin.'

Miss Allen looked puzzled. 'On Monday afternoon she suddenly began asking me odd questions.'

'Such as?'

'She wanted to know exactly where I'd been when that phone call came on Saturday night – and where I went later, after Susannah had left.'

'And where did you go?'

Miss Allen tossed her head. 'Here, there and everywhere. My position is no sinecure, you know. I have full responsibility for a great deal of valuable property, in financial terms as well as those of our cultural heritage. I was keeping an eye on the kitchen staff who were doing the refreshments and checking later that they'd cleared up properly. Then I had to make sure that none of the visitors had strayed into other parts of the house. The rooms were locked but we couldn't cut off the corridors and staircases.

'We had a security man on duty but he just made more work. I had to make sure he hadn't crept off for a sleep and to check that he was doing an occasional turn round the car park.'

'Sounds as though you were busy. Let's go back to Jane.'

Miss Allen sniffed. 'She was a silly, vain little thing.'

'*Nil nisi bonum* and so on?'

Miss Allen blushed unbecomingly and was silent.

When she felt the woman had been sufficiently rebuked, Jennie asked, 'Why should a girl like that want to work here?'

'It was a job.'

137

'Fair enough. Why did you take her on?'

Miss Allen admitted, reluctantly: 'She was better than some of the girls who presented themselves. Her appearance was good on the desk. She was shallow but she was quick and efficient. I didn't approve of her string of boyfriends or her social life in general but she didn't let them encroach on working time and she never chanced her arm with the visitors.'

'If that's how you felt about Jane, I'm surprised you weren't more shocked by Susannah's affairs.'

Miss Allen seemed unable to explain this anomaly to herself. She shook her head slowly. 'I was shocked, but as I told you we go back a long way. And there was something about Zannah. She swept you along with her.'

She paused, fidgeting with the pens in the tray on the desk. 'I miss Jane more than I'd have expected. She was a cheerful little soul most of the time. Her scornful attitude to what she called this mausoleum kept my worship of the past in proportion. Occasionally, I've quoted her forthright comments on the way of life of the Smithson-Crossley family and collected a good laugh from my audience. And she was very good at dealing with the visitors' minor crises, old ladies overcome by the heat or children suffering from a surfeit of sweets could always be left to her.'

The fiddling hands were suddenly still and Miss Allen looked directly at Jennie. 'Do you think she died just because she took that phone call?'

Jennie shrugged. 'I don't know. Did Jane say what she wanted to tell Sergeant Hunter?'

Miss Allen nodded. 'Yes, although I'm not sure how much help it would have been to him.' The song Miss Allen mentioned as the background to the call Jane Griffin had taken meant nothing to Jennie. Miss Allen obligingly hummed the tune till she was interrupted by her young visitor's clapping.

She smiled at him as he came forward. 'We enjoyed

your performance too, and the constable's.' Seeing that the two officers had more questions to ask, she found Luke another sorting job and dispatched him to the nether regions. 'I'm dying for some coffee. I could slip through and have it ready in a couple of minutes if you wouldn't mind staying here and giving me a call if someone comes.'

At Mitchell's nod of assent, she opened the door to the kitchen, leaving it ajar and calling through, 'It's quiet today as you can see. On Monday it was heaving. Hundreds of gawpers came to see the bloodstains on the bus shelter and then came on up here to justify the trip.'

She returned in little more than the promised two minutes and examined the photographs Mitchell passed to her as she drank her own coffee. 'That's Adam Holroyd, of course. If the dark-skinned one is Urfan Singh, then I can well understand why Susannah fell for him.' She looked up at Mitchell. 'Do I gather you're showing me the four possible fathers? I've never seen this one.' She handed back the picture of Hanson, then studied the last one for almost a minute. The two officers waited patiently. At last, she put it down on the desk. 'I'm sure he was one of Monday's gawpers, but he didn't look quite like that. He was tattier, somehow, although he was clean and tidily dressed.'

'How about nine or ten years older?'

'Yes, that's it. Men don't change very much between thirty and mid-fifties, just fray round the edges a bit.'

'You'd be prepared to swear to this man's having visited the hall on Monday?'

Miss Allen drank the rest of her coffee, considering. 'No, but I want to help. I'd be prepared to go wherever he is and have another look at him. I suppose you want to know when he was here?' When the officers nodded, she closed her eyes, trying to recapture the scene. 'It was about three o'clock. It was frantically busy here. I was only on the desk because the queue was longer than Jane could deal with. This chap was seven or eight places back but when I came to help, he jumped across to be first in my queue and totally ignored all the glares, so I had a good look at him.'

'Did he say anything?'

She shook her head. 'Not a lot. He bought one of the guides, wanted to know if the craft weekend had gone well and then asked the queue in general if anyone had visited it. A woman behind said she had and they went off together . . . Oh, he knew about the body being found. He was saying to the woman what a pity it was that it had given a nasty flavour to a pleasant event.'

'Did he know that it was Susannah?'

She shook her head again. 'I was dealing with the next person by then. I wasn't really listening. The TV news called her Susan. Maybe that's what he came to find out.' She began to collect their coffee cups on to a tray. Jennie and Mitchell put away notebooks and prepared to go.

As they reached the door, Miss Allen called them back. 'I've only just remembered. I passed through the foyer later, just as that man had finished the tour. He was deep in conversation with Jane.'

Chapter Thirteen

As Hunter drove into Sheffield that afternoon, past Western Park and the university, the small puddles in the gutters from the morning rain were gently steaming, though the sky was a clear cold blue. These conditions prevailed only in October, and only on the best days of that month, warmth with an underlying crispness that took over from mid-afternoon.

Now, at approaching one thirty, dog walkers sauntered through the park over neatly cut grass. Wasn't Sheffield famous for its city parks as well as its steel works?

Hunter thought the next right turn would be Jonathan Milton's street. As he came to it, he found the sign largely obscured. He parked and got out, opened the passenger door for Caroline, then lifted a heavy curtain of Virginia creeper in order to read it. They paused to admire the contrasting green and fiery red leaves that fell back over it before walking to the nearest wrought-iron gate in the stone wall and discovering they were standing outside Milton's house.

It was the end one of a grand terrace, built of blackened sandstone, relieved with sparkling white paint and glinting glass. It had windows on three sides so the inside would be huge and light. Hunter counted them. If the back of the house had the same number as the front, then there must be well over a dozen rooms on three floors. Nice!

He rang the bell and they were immediately admitted into the wide, wood-panelled hallway. The ceiling there, painted hyacinth blue, gave the impression that it was open to the sky. On the wall, to his left, hung a neat row of Heaton Cooper watercolours of the Lake District. Hunter looked closely at the nearest and saw that it was not a print.

Hunter and PC Webster had been let in by a middle-aged woman of the twinset and tweeds variety who introduced herself as Sheila Milton's secretary. Obviously the householders were not anxious to be seen admitting the law. From the inside, the house proved to be even bigger than Hunter had imagined it. The ground floor seemed to consist of offices. As they waited, the secretary flitted in and out through the various doors.

Presently, Milton came down the curved staircase to meet them. Hunter approved of his appearance. He was a healthy-looking specimen in his late fifties, lean, and tanned by the wind and sun rather than by a lamp, Hunter thought. His skin was slightly rough and weather-beaten. He had made no attempt to disguise his receding hairline, his teeth were good and his hands, one resting lightly on the banister, were well cared for. He wore navy slacks and a light blue, heavy-knit jacket with suede shoulders. He had dignified the occasion with a white shirt and a university tie.

He shook hands with each of them and suggested that their business should be transacted in his study. Hunter imagined a cosy box with a desk and two or three chairs. The room they entered merited a conducted tour.

Milton answered Hunter's unspoken comment. 'I use it for tutorials and, sometimes, for departmental meetings. It's more relaxed and comfortable than my university office.'

Hunter sat down but didn't speak, taking in the details of his surroundings. Milton, uncomfortable with the silence, filled it. 'I've been in this post two years now – and in this house too.'

Satisfied that his man was rattled, Hunter began his

interview. 'I want to go eight years further back than that. What sort of student was Susannah Farrar?'

He smiled and made no pretence of having to search his memory. 'Very pretty, very bright, even brilliant on occasion, but unpredictable. I don't think she went as far as she might have done after college. She wasn't exactly lazy but she was unfocused. She had great and sudden enthusiasms, tried to pack half a lifetime into her three years.'

'And when did you last see her?'

He answered promptly. 'Ten years ago last June, on degree presentation day.'

'And her friends?'

He spread his fingers out on his knees and regarded them fixedly. 'Many and various. She was a lively and sociable student. She had lots of friends. I've seen none of them, to my knowledge, since the same day.'

Hunter's voice sharpened. 'We happen to know otherwise.'

Milton's fingers twitched but his manner was urbane. 'Then I've obviously overlooked something, Sergeant, but you'll have to remind me. It obviously wasn't anything sufficiently significant for me to waste your time by recalling it.'

'I believe you had a recent contact with Mr Matthew Hanson.'

'Oh, yes.' He looked rueful.

'Well?'

'To my shame, on that occasion I got rather inebriated. Perhaps that's why my subconscious wanted to block it out. It was about a month ago. I hardly ever drink so a very little can go to my head.'

'Did you meet by arrangement?'

He shook his head. 'Sheila and I were in Birmingham. There's another by-election coming up there. Sheila has stood against the socialist candidate in that constituency three times counting this one. Recently, she was offered

143

a safer seat but she'd cut down the Labour man's majority so much, she felt it would give her more satisfaction to win this one when the present member retires.

'The social whirl it involves was getting tedious – for me at any rate – so I'd gone off for an evening on my own away from it. I met Hanson by chance in the bar of the Grapes of Wrath. Hanson stays there when he has business in Birmingham.'

'I'm surprised,' Hunter remarked, conversationally, 'that his phone call yesterday hadn't caused your meeting with him to be fresh in your mind. I'd like your version of it.'

'Phone call? From Hanson?'

'When Constable Mitchell pressed Mr Hanson's re-dial button, you politely enquired what you could do to help him.'

Milton shrugged. 'All right. He suggested another meeting. I didn't fancy repeating the occasion. I'm no drinker, as I said. From my recollection of him as a student, I hadn't thought he was either.'

'I see.' Hunter's voice was toneless. He stared at Caroline. Caroline scribbled busily in shorthand. Milton displayed signs of anxiety. Suddenly, Hunter addressed him again. 'Had you heard about the death of Susannah Farrar?'

'So it *was* Zannah? I feared it might be.'

'Is that why you visited Crossley Hall on Monday?'

Milton sighed. 'The TV news said the girl's name was Susan. I thought, if Farrar was a local name there was just a chance that it might not be.'

'Why did it matter to you?'

'Be reasonable, Sergeant. I wanted to know for old times' sake, because she'd been a good student, and I could follow my fancy and go because of the glorious freedom of a sabbatical.'

'The hall is worth a visit for its own sake,' Hunter remarked.

'Yes, a nice old place.' Milton's tone echoed the sergeant's.

'You bought a guide book, I hear.'

Milton looked startled. 'No harm in that, is there?'

'None. What did you talk about to Jane Griffin?'

'Who?'

'The girl on the desk.'

'The fat one, or the young, pretty one?'

'The latter.'

Milton shrugged. 'This and that. I just made myself pleasant.'

'Did you mention Susannah?'

'We did, actually. The girl knew her. We were both saying how sorry . . .'

'You were sorry?'

'Well, of course.'

'You didn't feel just a slight relief that the drain on your income had stopped? You didn't feel a slight degree of satisfaction that the girl had got her come-uppance after nine years of blackmailing you and Hanson and Singh and Holroyd?'

'Singh and Holroyd?' A variety of emotions was reflected in Milton's face.

Hunter added to his discomfiture. 'Sorry to keep springing surprises on you. But perhaps it won't be a surprise to hear that, after being observed in close conversation with you, Jane Griffin was not seen again until her body was discovered on Tuesday. Now, perhaps you can concentrate harder on what you both said.'

Hunter turned up first at the Thursday morning briefing. 'Jennie's just arriving and Benny's downstairs. He's in a bad mood,' he warned Browne, 'because they gave him a hard time in court yesterday afternoon and his pimp got off.'

Browne was annoyed. He had invested a good deal of time and manpower in the case and a clever piece of detection on Mitchell's part had nailed their man. 'It was probably his own fault. His cocky manner always puts people's backs up. It's no good being a whiz at "nicking", to use his favourite expression, if he can't back up his own work in court.'

Hunter was more tolerant. 'Wigmore is always lenient and Benny is better than he used to be. His manners haven't improved a lot on the surface but his uncouthness is mostly tongue in cheek now. He doesn't want to lose face by abandoning his boorish behaviour, but he's sufficiently ashamed of it to mock himself.'

Browne laughed. 'You're right, and I usually know better than to criticize one officer to another. I shall be nice to him this morning to compensate.'

Jennie and Mitchell came in and settled themselves and Browne began the morning's business. 'The good news is that, seeing as this is the most serious case on the stocks at present, now there's been a second killing, Superintendent Petty has drafted in a small army of DCs and uniformed men – at least, compared with what we've been managing with – to help with routine. The bad news is that, as well as all the people who might resent or dislike someone in the ordinary run of things, our first victim has been deliberately cheating at least four men. Four men, moreover, who seem to have found her out, with the possible exception of Holroyd. Then we have another death which we believe to be connected with the first. What now?'

Jennie beat Mitchell with her suggestion. 'We've spent most of our time so far on the four men. Who else is there?'

'There's the family,' Hunter contributed. 'I suppose we can count the parents out, so let's see if we can eliminate the rest. Mrs Wilson was at work. The day shift goes off at nine fifteen and it takes her twenty minutes to get there. Her husband collected her the next morning, leaving the old lady in their daughter's charge for a few minutes. We've not really considered Mr Wilson yet.'

146

Browne nodded. 'Your job for this morning, then. Benny?'

Mitchell scowled in concentration. 'We need to find out something about the people Susannah worked for but I haven't many suggestions about how to track them down. I suppose we'll have to go back to all the gubbins from the bank and trace the cheques paid in. And we might get a bit more out of Wendy Allen, if we can believe what she says.'

'Jennie?'

'I'm going to change my mind and stick with the four men. We can talk to the other businessmen at Singh's conference, check with Hanson's parents and sister, ask questions of all Sheila Milton's associates.'

'The professor isn't going to like that.'

Browne was undismayed. 'None of them will, I suppose. By the way, we haven't shown the photographs to Julie Wilson. Any of the four could have approached her in some way without her knowing who they were. Jerry, can you do that when you go to see the husband?'

'I can try, but those two seem to have to take it in turns to be in.'

'What concerns me,' Browne observed, 'is that all the four who were being blackmailed might be in collusion.'

'I don't think so.'

Browne grinned. 'Go on, Jerry, I want to believe you.'

'Well, not in Milton's case, anyway. He practically admitted that he and Hanson knew they were both being conned, but I'd swear that he was genuinely astonished when he realized she'd been fleecing Holroyd and Singh as well. That doesn't make him innocent, of course. He was the only one of them who was around on Monday.'

'That we know about.' Hunter nodded.

Jennie's head re-emerged from the wings of the armchair. 'Milton didn't behave on Monday like a man with something to hide. Wendy Allen says he drew attention to himself by queue-jumping, and then he stood for a while in the foyer for all to see, chatting with Jane.'

Hunter got up and prowled again. 'I wonder what Jane told him. Perhaps something she said made him think she was a danger to him and he only decided he had to get rid of her after that. He admitted she told him she was going to see me after work with some important information. He claims she wouldn't tell him what it was.'

'Just a minute,' Mitchell demanded. 'Are you for or against him?'

Hunter shook his head. 'I don't know.'

'Maybe,' Browne suggested, 'the high profile was the whole point.'

'One of the others sneaks in you mean, whilst Milton draws attention to himself, knowing that he's spent his whole visit chatting to other visitors who'll vouch for him when we've searched them out?' Mitchell paused for them to digest this convoluted question.

'If only we could all catch on so quickly!'

They all looked at Jennie in astonishment and she withdrew to the depths of the armchair.

Mitchell, unabashed, continued. 'Most of what we've got about the hall on Monday is only what Wendy Allen told us. She could have made it all up. Maybe that tune wasn't the background to the Saturday phone call. Maybe the real piece of information Jane was going to give us was something that would incriminate her. She's the only one who has a close connection with both victims.'

There was an exclamation of annoyance from the armchair. 'I've just remembered something I forgot to follow up. Wendy Allen was talking about the problems Susannah was going to have explaining the reduction in her income when Luke got too old for maintenance. She said that's why she refused to do something but your recorder recital distracted her before she'd said what it was – or rather, she used it as the excuse for not finishing something she hadn't intended to say.'

'Recorder recital, Benny?' There was a glint in Hunter's eye.

148

Mitchell glowered, first at Jennie, then at him.

'Pity we can't get Richard to frighten it out of her,' Jennie continued quickly, hoping to rescue Mitchell.

Browne's heart sank. Mitchell was unlikely to be soothed by a reference to Richard Dean's promotion to detective sergeant in the North Yorkshire force, an appointment he would have been qualified to apply for himself if it were not for his family responsibilities. 'Let's get some more footwork done then,' he suggested hurriedly.

Mitchell's action sheet dispatched him first to see Mrs Wheway, Susannah Farrar's daily cleaner, before sending him on a second trip to York. He would do the local job as quickly as possible and then go home for a peaceful cup of coffee with his wife. When the alarm had rung this morning they had both turned over for an extra ten minutes' sleep, thanking providence that it was Thursday again. The previous year it had been the day when Virginia had had four consecutive morning lectures and the domestic problems had been solved by Mitchell's mother picking up her grandson the previous evening and keeping him till the following afternoon. Both grandparents and child had approved of the arrangement, which had continued after the need for it had passed.

Cheered by the prospect of rehearsing his grievances to his wife, Mitchell set off for the Westclough Estate. Mrs Wheway's house was a good advertisement for her services, its garden unimaginative but neat even in the late autumn and its paintwork sparkling. She was waiting to receive him, as were several of her neighbours, who regarded him curiously and made no pretence of having any outdoor task to perform. She gave a wave of acknowledgement to her audience, then swept inside, like the prime minister entering number ten, with Mitchell in her wake.

She needed no prompting to begin her story. 'A man came to see Miss Farrar Saturday morning.'

'What were you doing there?' Mitchell asked her.

'My weekend whip-round, of course. Saw him drive up and park outside number four while she was still in.' She shared a dramatic pause with Mitchell, her button eyes fixed on his face.

'Miss Farrar went out then?' Mitchell prompted after some moments.

'That's right. Took the boy shopping. Soon as she'd disappeared round the corner he climbs out and comes to the door, making out how sorry he is to have missed her.'

'What did you make of that?'

She pushed her face into Mitchell's conspiratorially. 'I thought he might be a private detective. She's on the game if you ask me.'

'And what did this caller ask you?'

'He asked me plenty.'

'Did you tell him plenty?'

She shook her head. 'I could have. I don't·miss much but I can't stand nosy folk.'

'It's my job to be nosy, I'm afraid.'

She laughed inordinately. 'Oh, you're different, Inspector.'

Mitchell ground his teeth. He'd never be anything but a constable at his present rate of progress. Having made Virginia pregnant during her first term at Oxford, he had to make sure that her studies were not too seriously interrupted. That, together with various domestic crises and his work, meant he had made little progress with his own advancement. Not that he had any real regrets. He had already been planning to marry Virginia and he would certainly not be without Declan. 'Just constable, I'm afraid,' he told Mrs Wheway. 'How much did you tell?'

She shrugged. 'Just that she wasn't without a bob or two, that she wasn't in much, that the boy went to a posh school. I showed him Luke's room. Shouldn't have, I suppose.'

'And what did he say he'd come for?'

'Said he wanted to see her. Old university friend. Hadn't much time to spare. Where was she? I told him I didn't know, but in the afternoon she was going to Crossley Hall. Luke had told me about it.'

'And would you know him again?'

She tossed her head. 'Course I would. I was talking to him for more than half an hour.'

Mitchell took out his Xeroxed pictures and handed her one.

'Not him!' She was indignant. 'I wouldn't have told a black man where to find her!' Mitchell warmed to her. If people had prejudices he preferred it when they were not coy about them.

She reached for the remaining three photographs and examined them. 'Are these all her fancy men?'

'Just tell me if the man you spoke to is one of them.'

She pointed with a chapped finger. 'Yes, it's him, the bald one. Not much to look at, is he? Must be her sugar daddy.'

Chapter Fourteen

By eleven Mitchell was seated opposite his wife at his own kitchen table, being called to account for his black mood. He wasn't sure he could explain it himself. The court case still rankled. He'd taken stick from Hunter about playing the child's recorder, but what was wrong with him if something so trivial depressed him? 'Jennie wishes Richard were back,' he told Virginia, surprising himself.

'So you're jealous of Richard and I suppose you blame me?'

'Why should I blame you? Anyway, no, I'm not. I want what he's got but I don't begrudge it him. Actually, I miss him.'

Virginia sniffed. 'You didn't seem so fond of him when he was here. You were always arguing and insulting one another.'

Mitchell sighed. 'That's the whole point. He didn't care what I thought so I could say anything I liked. Now I'm always pussy-footing about with touchy people, having to watch my tongue all the time.'

She was indignant. 'My father isn't touchy!'

'No, but he is my boss.'

She poured him a cup of her diabolical coffee. 'Tell me about the case.'

'You know most of it.'

'I know the facts. Tell me about the people.'

He swallowed the brown liquid with a deadpan face.

'There's a woman in charge of the whole set-up at Crossley Hall, called Wendy Allen. She's a great fat slug of a woman . . .'

'So you want the culprit to be her?'

He laughed. 'I suppose I do. I have to admit she's good with the boy, though. Things were piling up against Jonathan Milton this morning.'

'What's he like?'

Mitchell shrugged. 'Haven't met him but I gather he's been a bit of a lad in his time.'

Virginia set her cup down. 'Why is my coffee so awful?' Mitchell knew better than to answer that. 'I don't think it'll turn out to be one of the four men. I don't believe anyone would kill purely for revenge with nothing to gain except the satisfaction of getting their own back. It's cutting off your nose, etc. They'd have too much to lose. They might sue her and get some of their money back, perhaps . . .'

'That's because you're not vindictive and you haven't got a violent temper.'

Virginia shook her head. 'This wasn't done in a rage. Not by one of those four anyway. All the travelling and careful timing it would take would have to be carefully planned.' As Mitchell's hand felt for the biscuit tin for the third time she removed it beyond his reach. 'You've had two. Don't tell me you'll convert them to muscle at your rugby practice. You can't make muscle out of carbohydrate and fat. If you're really hungry we could have an early lunch. There's still half the shepherd's pie from yesterday. I could microwave it in a couple of minutes.'

Mitchell considered that disposing of the first half had been over and above the call of duty. 'Thanks but I've got a packet of sarnies in the car. I've got to be in York in just over an hour. I've stayed too long already.' He kissed the top of her head. 'Thanks for cheering me up.'

What had she said? Was he being . . .? No, irony was not in Benny's repertoire.

*

153

The wind was getting up as Hunter climbed out of his car. It took the driver's door out of his loose grip and clanged it back against the front wing. The resulting noise was such that when he examined his old Morris 1000 he was thankful the small dent and minor scratches were no worse. That would teach him to cling sentimentally to his much cherished first and only car. The hinges of modern ones locked long before the doors could swing far enough back to damage a wing.

'Mr Kevin Wilson?' he enquired of the man in his thirties who opened the door to him before he could knock. The man nodded, finger to his lips, and admitted Hunter, who obligingly crept inside. Mr Wilson's face, Hunter thought, might have been handsome if the world had treated it better, but its features were not sufficiently classic to take the closely cropped hairstyle. The hair, if it had been allowed, would have grown dark and the scalp looked as if it had been well peppered. The nose was large and well shaped, the lips thick, and the jaw, at nine thirty in the morning, had a five o'clock shadow. Maybe Mr Wilson's daily shave was after tea rather than before breakfast because, in the days before his mother-in-law's stay, it had been more important to look tidy for an evening out than for a day spent tinkering with machinery.

He wore jeans and a once-black, much washed T-shirt covered by a flowered apron. His expression was good-natured. He led Hunter to the kitchen, which he seemed to fill, and resumed his duties at the sink. Hunter watched from the doorway. 'Lisa usually washes the breakfast dishes before she goes to school but Ma was more confused and awkward than usual this morning.' The voice was deep, Hunter noted. 'I'm just trying to tidy round now she's dozed off. It won't last long. She doesn't sleep much, night or day.'

'That must make life very difficult.'

Mr Wilson sighed. 'You can say that again. I don't suppose we could have done any different but I think

154

we've bitten off a bit more than we can chew.' He scraped bacon rind into the waste bin and immersed another stack of plates in the suds. 'It's not the hard work so much, it's the sex.'

Hunter wondered if he had heard aright. 'Did you say sex?' He took up a teacloth and began to dry plates, placing them soundlessly on the Formica table.

Mr Wilson nodded his thanks. 'Yes, and with the boys it's very awkward. The doc says it's all part of the disease.'

Gradually, with patient questioning, Hunter learned that one of the features of the later stages of Alzheimer's disease is an increased interest in sexual matters, sometimes after years of inactivity. 'And Ma was never one for all that business, even in her heyday.' Mrs Farrar was now in the inconvenient habit of making unmistakable overtures to inappropriate people. She also suffered from delusions about sexual relations between others. 'She accuses me and Lisa of awful things and sometimes exposes herself. Lisa's old enough to understand at least a bit but Steven gets very embarrassed and Wayne thinks it's hilarious. All three of them have stopped bringing their friends home over the last few weeks and I can understand why.'

Hunter could think of no consolatory answer and changed the subject. 'Is your wife in?'

'She is, but she's in bed. She was on duty last night. Sometimes she manages a short snooze if the old folks aren't troublesome but she's more usually awake all night. We've both got our shifts organized so I can hold the fort for a couple of hours after she gets in. I don't want to wake her unless your questions are really urgent.'

Hunter assured him that he would not dream of disturbing Mrs Wilson just yet.

'So what can I do for you?'

Hunter felt that the man's obvious integrity was his alibi but knew that neither his CI nor a court of law could accept this as evidence. He wondered how to extract the

155

answers he needed without offending the man and adding to his troubles, then decided to put his dilemma into words.

Mr Wilson understood. 'Sure, ask what you like.'

'Let's start with your job.'

Another raised finger warned Hunter to lower his voice again. 'I'm an engineer at the Yorkshire Provident Building Society HQ in Bradford. Their computers are going twenty-four hours a day. I'm a maintenance man.'

'And your hours?'

Mr Wilson grinned. 'Many and various. I'm quite popular with my employers because it suits me to do split shifts – what with the complicated arrangements at home.'

Hunter placed the last fork quietly on the table. 'How did the shifts work out between you on Saturday?'

He scratched his head, working it out. 'I did the nine o'clock till one. It meant that I could fetch Julie home at eight o'clock and she could have a couple of hours in bed because Lisa was in. She can cope if there are no emergencies and she can always call her mum if she needs to. When I came home I took the boys to football – they play in the Cloughton junior league. When I got back I had a bit of a kip myself. It's quieter when the boys aren't around but you can't relax. The old woman wanders and you have to watch and toilet her. Susan came with the bairn whilst I was asleep and she took Ma to the hospital to see Peter.'

'Your father-in-law?'

'S'right. Julie went to bed again. I wanted her to stay there but she came down when Sue got back. She doesn't come all that often and Julie likes to see her.'

Something in his tone struck Hunter. 'Did you like your sister-in-law?'

He sighed. 'I thought she was a complete cow but I rubbed along with her for Julie's sake and the old folks. I'm sorry for the bairn. He's a complete oddball, the result of his upbringing, but there's no harm in him.' Mr

Wilson perched on a kitchen stool and invited Hunter to do likewise. 'Lord knows what'll happen to him now, but I can't let Julie take him. Our family's under enough pressure as it is.'

'What happened later on Saturday, in the evening?'

Searching his memory necessitated more head scratching. 'I took Julie to work at nine o'clock. Lisa covered for me again. We got the boys to bed as soon as I got back and Lisa entertained Ma, playing tapes to her. She likes music. Then we got her to bed between us and Lisa and I had supper. It's a rotten life for a twelve-year-old, she's old before her time. Anyway, then we both got our heads down but with half an ear cocked. Ma only got up once, Saturday, but the bed was wet and we had to change it. I'd rather have coped on my own but Lisa's a light sleeper and she just appeared as I was doing it. She made some tea.'

'What time was this?'

'About midnight or just after.'

Hunter apologized for requiring the same sort of detail about the following Monday and he produced a similar recital of tiresome and trivial duties. 'Julie was out a lot, at the hall seeing about the boy, and then shopping. I picked her up at the supermarket about six o'clock. I didn't want her to go to work. She looked really worn out. I took Monday as my day off. Will you be much longer? I'm on at twelve o'clock today and I want to take the vacuum cleaner round before then.'

Hunter quickly produced his photographs. Kevin Wilson glanced at them briefly, shaking his head at each in turn until he came to the picture of Urfan Singh. 'I know that bloke. He's in computers, though I'm not sure exactly what he does. He often visits my boss and comes out looking like the cat that's stolen the cream, so I suppose we buy from him. You don't think he bumped Susan off?'

Hunter shrugged. 'Who knows?'

157

There was a scrabbling at the living-room door and Mr Wilson leapt up to investigate. As he opened it an old woman came through, eyed Hunter speculatively, then lifted her woollen skirt to reveal shrunken thighs. She dropped it again quickly and wiped her hand on her cardigan. 'Why have you put me in wet clothes?'

Her son-in-law groaned. 'All right, come on, Ma, let's get 'em off.'

Hunter thought that if this man was going to commit murder he would do it closer to home than the vicinity of Crossley Hall. 'Isn't there an institution where she could go?' he asked quietly. 'Somewhere you could all visit often?'

Kevin Wilson grimaced. 'There's the local council place. She might qualify for an allowance to be taken there – although nothing's certain any more – but Julie would never agree. She knows about these things and she says that one's awful, not like the nice private place where she works. That's out of the question for us though. Peter's still talking about when he can take over again. He knows that his cancer is terminal but he hasn't accepted it. What he doesn't know is how bad Ma has got. It doesn't show so much in short visits.'

Hunter left his photographs behind for Julie Wilson to look at. 'Ask her to ring me if she recognizes any of them.' He departed, leaving Wilson to attend to his mother-in-law.

Outside, Hunter opened his car door carefully, holding it firmly against the minor gale that was blowing. Distracted by a click, he looked up to see a young girl in the gateway of the house he had just left. Gleefully, as his hand loosened its grip on the door, the wind tore it away, this time pinning him between it and the already dented wing.

He rarely swore and was prevented this time by finding the girl beside him. 'Are you all right?'

He assured her he was unhurt. 'You must be Lisa.' She nodded. 'Not at school today?'

She grinned at him. 'Not any more. Burst water pipe. The loos don't work and there's not going to be any dinner, so we've packed up for the day.'

'You don't look too worried. Are your brothers being sent home too?'

She shook her head. 'They're still at the junior school, thank goodness.' She was looking at him doubtfully.

He produced his warrant card to reassure her, and she examined it with great interest. 'I've been talking to your father about your aunt.'

'Auntie Sue? You won't have heard anything good about her then.'

A more scrupulous officer in many ways than Mitchell, Hunter refused to follow up this opening, remarking instead, 'You look as though you could do with an after-noon's rest. Your father tells me your grandmother has been giving you both some disturbed nights.'

The girl nodded. 'She's been awful this week except Saturday. She only had us up once then and of course that would be the night poor old dad got routed out by his firm.'

This was more than Hunter could resist. 'That was bad luck.'

She shrugged. 'In a way, but he was quite proud, too, you know, that it was something only he could fix. He sneaked out without calling me and hoping both me and Gran would stay asleep, but I heard both the phone and the car. I wake very easily. He must have fixed things quickly. He wasn't away long.'

'Was it before your gran woke, or after?'

She screwed up her nose. 'It was before. We were just dropping off to sleep again when I heard her scratching at the door. I'd just got warm and stayed in bed, but when I heard him groping about I felt mean so I got up and made some tea. I'd better get in. Not knowing I'm here, he'll wake Mum up soon.' She waved as Hunter drew away.

Hunter waved back, vowing that in future he would

159

bear more charitably, even thankfully, the intelligent interference of both his parents and Annette's.

On the days when his daughter's prefectorial duties included keeping a sharp watch on the queue for the school buses, James Smith dropped Vanessa off at the point as near to the bus station as his route to his office allowed him. She scrambled out of the car, glad to stretch her legs. It was a sunny Friday morning and Cloughton was a pleasant town. She was glad they'd moved here. She much preferred it to dirty, bustling Leeds. The shops were good in spite of being fitted into old Victorian buildings. The council had built new ones in between but they were quite in keeping with the old stuff, and some clever architect had linked the old and the new in the main precinct by giving all the buildings a uniform wrought-iron and glass canopy.

Vanessa crossed the central fan-design of the cobbles to have another look at the jacket she coveted in the window of River Island. Then she increased her pace, dodging and weaving, hoping that she'd reach the bus station no later than Mark, who shared her duty.

Really, she was beginning rather to fancy Mark. He was clever, interesting to talk to. She actually liked discussing their work now they were well on with A-levels. She had been flattered when Ian had picked her out at the disco. At twenty-five he had seemed sophisticated, a man of the world. He had money in his pocket and it was quite exciting, tearing around on the back of his motorbike – and she'd felt so adult when he'd taken her to bed. But Ian was really fairly boring when he had all his clothes on, which, when you thought about it, was most of the time.

The bus station was in sight now, the roof of its paper shop and coffee bar glinting against the scruffy green and hazy skyline across the valley, its lamps like giant bell flowers. She saw, to her relief, that Mark was just approaching from the opposite direction. They met in the newsagent's doorway and Vanessa went in to buy a music magazine. She came out with it under her arm and a frown on her face. 'They're selling lottery tickets in there to loads of folk in school uniforms. Think we should check for any of ours?'

Mark shook his head. 'We can't do an age check on them all and if they're fifth-formers over sixteen they're not doing anything wrong.'

They stationed themselves at the top of the thirty-degree slope that was the bus station and kept half an eye on the as-yet straggling queue of children waiting for the 606 to Heath Lees School. 'I love those green and cream single-deckers. They're big and fat and friendly.' Vanessa bit her tongue. What a stupid remark. Why did she have to say such silly things whenever she liked a boy?

Mark replied, politely enough, 'It says something for their engines that they always manage the hill start to get them out of here, even in the worst of weather.' Vanessa smiled to herself. That wasn't a typical example of Mark's conversation. Was he feeling shy with her, too?

They stood silently, watching alternately the scurrying of passengers and the hillside opposite, where buses that had left the station some minutes earlier could be seen snaking their way towards the outer edges of civilization halfway up.

'I'm glad we're not responsible for that lot.' Mark indicated the queue at the end platform where pupils from the school at the other end of the town amused themselves somersaulting over restraining bars, leaping across bus lanes just as vehicles were pulling away, shinning up any vertical structures and generally being obstreperous.

Vanessa grinned. 'Don't speak too soon.' She indicated the approach road where two notorious characters from their own year ten were pushing each other and smoking.

The two prefects decided the approach road was

161

outside their jurisdiction. Their brief was to make sure the behaviour of the Heath Lees bus queue was seemly. Her recent visit to the Cloughton mortuary had cured Vanessa of any unnecessary interference in other people's affairs.

Mark pulled a face. 'I hope those two don't stray into the coffee bar. The old dragon in there stirs up trouble, issuing threats before anyone's even put a foot wrong, and now they get a kick out of defying her. Have you started your history essay?'

Vanessa nodded. 'I've done a fair bit of reading, but I haven't got down to writing anything yet. How about you?'

Mark laughed. 'The opposite.'

'You've written it without reading anything?'

'Well, I've made a start. Kendrew is always on about defining your terms so that's provided me with one and a half pages. "James the First, the wisest fool in Christendom" – a paragraph each on what is wisdom (for a king), what's foolish (ditto), and how much of civilization is meant by "Christendom".'

'Let me look at that and I'll give you my notes from the Early Stuarts.' They grinned conspiratorially.

Mark touched her arm. 'There's Paul Kelly all over that new blonde year-eleven girl from down south somewhere.' They watched, in Vanessa's case with mixed feelings. Doing this duty kept you up to date with the latest gossip, but what was being said about her and Mark?

Suddenly she grasped Mark's forearm so that her fingers bit through even the firm fabric of his blazer. Startled, he turned to her and saw that he was merely the recipient of her manifest excitement and not the cause of it. Her eyes were following the progress of one of the figures moving across the striped area of the bus lane reserved for pedestrians to cross. Seeing no one there he recognized, he gazed down at her white knuckles, a little embarrassed. 'What's up? Seen a ghost?'

162

Vanessa, unaware that he had spoken, kept her eyes fixed on the fair-haired woman who had alighted from the bus in number five bay on C platform. She had now reached A and was making for a number below four since she had turned right. She was quite sure this was the woman she had driven to the hospital on Saturday night. She felt none of the agony of indecision she had experienced on examining that other woman's dead face. She must catch up with her, ask her how she was feeling, get her name, tell her the police needed her assistance.

Mark took her wrist and tried to loosen her grip on his forearm. 'Come on, this is the last bus. Time to ride with the villains. Thank goodness it's over for another week.'

There wasn't time to explain. Vanessa sprinted down platform B, across to A and turned right as the woman had done. Mark's indignant voice floated after her. In quick succession she saw the fair woman clinging to the platform rail of the 401 as it moved out of bay A2, and her own school bus lumbering out of B7, carrying an extremely angry looking Mark.

'Damn, damn, damn!'

Chapter Fifteen

Mitchell distracted himself from Virginia's lumpy Friday-morning porridge by going over in his mind the salient points of his interview in York the previous afternoon. His session with George Hanson and his wife had made Mitchell less contemptuous of their son. Mr Hanson senior had managed to put as many questions as he had received and in return for the facts he had discovered Mitchell had had to reveal that he was, nominally, a Roman Catholic. (Bad news, this. The Pope was an anathema to George Hanson's sect and he obviously considered Mitchell to have less chance of salvation than an infidel.) Furthermore, he had admitted, with some embarrassment, that his mother had obliged him to attend Sunday School long enough to become acquainted with some of the notorious anti-heroes of Old Testament fame. And that, in spite of this, he had not capitulated and embraced the Hansons' way of life and thinking.

The old man feared for such hardness of heart and such present neglect of Bible reading, and almost despaired to hear that, at two years old, Mitchell's son was not familiar with the inside of a church – apart, that is, from his baptism and one disastrous attempt to hush him during a family marriage ceremony. Hanson promised to pray daily for the constable and his family.

Mitchell could now empathize to some degree with the son who had bent to his earthly father's will, less because he feared being disinherited than because he could not summon up the energy for the daily fight. At the same time he felt a reluctant admiration for the father. Less, though, for his wife, who sat nodding and murmuring her agreement with each sentiment expressed by her earthly lord. She reminded Mitchell of the members of the cabinet and shadow cabinet flanking their party leader when he spoke from the front bench, sycophantically neighing their agreement.

The house seemed to the DC to have something of the dignity of the Houses of Parliament, but softened by deep carpets, restful colours and elegant flower arrangements. Substituting for old masters on the wall were gilt-framed exhortations and promises in italic script. He had tried not to smile at the one in the dining room – a jungle of greenery with numerous rubber plants – 'they that sow in tears shall reap in joy'. He thought it unlikely that much of the sowing, indoors or out, had been done by the elderly couple who would enjoy the results.

But the message in the entrance hall pleased him. 'The eternal God is thy refuge and underneath are the everlasting arms.' He decided he rather liked it. It answered Hanson's disparaging remarks about Roman Catholics.

Mitchell had managed to extract a confirmation that on Saturday last, both Matthew and Grace had attended 'a little supper party to give thanks for thirty-two years of Christian marriage'. Watching the cooking time of various dishes had caused Mrs Hanson to be certain that her first guest arrived too early at a minute after seven and her children on time at seven fifteen. They had arrived and left together, rather early, 'quite soon after Mrs Grant, my housekeeper, had finished serving the coffee, actually.' Mitchell hoped aloud that no incident had occurred to spoil the celebration. 'Not really, Constable. It's just that Grace is a very busy doctor and she was called away quite soon after the meal was over. She was driving Matt because he had carelessly left his car lights on early that morning and in the evening had found that his battery

165

was quite flat. Our other guests were two couples who are close neighbours who had walked to the house so it seemed the best solution for Matt.'

Mitchell had asked what the time was when the party was broken up in this way, but both the Hansons shook their heads, smiling. 'It wasn't broken up. We oldies went on chatting and drinking coffee for some time. We'd stopped worrying about the meal and therefore about the time, though I know the young folk had been gone some little while when our friends finally left at about midnight.'

'Rather late for us,' Mrs Hanson added, 'but it was a special occasion.'

As Mitchell took his leave, he rashly commented on the name of the house, 'Peniel', neatly painted on a wooden plaque. 'Is it a place you've visited together?' They laughed merrily. 'It's a spiritual place we've visited.' Mitchell backed impatiently towards his car as Mr Hanson treated him to the section of Genesis that dealt with Jacob's wrestling with the Lord. He delivered his punch line through the wound-down window. 'And Jacob called the name of the place Peniel, "for I have seen God face to face and my life is preserved".'

'Good story,' Mitchell said fatuously, turning his key in the ignition and hurriedly driving away. He had managed to obtain Grace Hanson's address. He hoped that, being a doctor, she would have her feet planted firmly in the present world.

Mitchell began to suspect Grace Hanson's evidence from the moment he discovered her brother was in her house. Not, he admitted to himself, that there was anything wrong in that. The twins were no more alike than any siblings. Grace was tall, possibly half an inch taller than her brother, and he had the impression that she managed him.

A meaningful glance from her ordered him away and he disappeared into her kitchen. Her tone when she

166

addressed Mitchell was not friendly. 'I gather I'm required to confirm that my brother and I dutifully attended a sedate dinner party on the occasion of our parents' wedding anniversary last Saturday.' He was not sure whether her animosity was against her brother for having made himself vulnerable, her parents for boring her, or himself. It suited him to let her conduct the interview as she had planned and he sat down, uninvited, to listen.

'We were rewarded with bountiful supplies of good food for playing the parts of grateful, loving offspring to an audience of such of our parents' friends as would appreciate and envy this devotion. We kept it up from seven fifteen until nine thirty when our pre-arranged rescue was effected by a call on my cellphone that summoned me to the bedside of a mythical mother. The complicated birth of her premature twins was fabricated on Friday. We also arranged that Matt would run down his battery.' She put a hand to her head as a noise of falling crockery came from the kitchen. 'My parents would not find it difficult to believe that Matt had accidentally managed to disable his car. Since he was my passenger, we left together at about twenty-five to ten with profuse thanks and apologies.'

'You took him to his house?' She nodded. 'So he was alone from when?'

'Not until after midnight. I invited myself in for a nightcap and we spent a maudlin hour and a half reviewing our childhood over a couple of brandies. We needed the first one.' Mitchell noticed that the aggressive note had left her voice and she was merely remembering aloud. 'After an evening's sycophancy the atmosphere between us was one of faint embarrassment as we each sought remarks that would restore our normal frankness. Isn't it amazing that they can still do that to us?' Matt came in from the kitchen and dispensed tea.

'It was slightly more tolerable than last time.' Grace had gone on speaking without looking at him.

167

Matt grinned as he handed her a cup. 'It made a great difference, knowing it was finite and that the phone would ring. Why do we keep going through this silly charade?' Delighted that they seemed to be absorbed in each other, Mitchell endeavoured to withdraw himself.

'Because the old dears need it more than we need to rebel,' Grace decided, adding quantities of sugar to her tea.

Matt stirred his own cup morosely. 'You've never found the need to rebel. I've never found the courage.'

'Oh, nonsense, Matt.' She laughed and turned back to Mitchell. 'We were cunning to make our story about twins. It always disarms them. They identify. Matt and I arrived only ten months after their wedding. Doubtless Father thanked the Lord for His abundance and Mother thanked Him, equally fervently, because He had enabled her to provide Father with both a son to carry on the family name and the family business, and a daughter to dress up and display, with only the inconvenience of a single pregnancy.

'With her duty so quickly and easily done, she saved Father the guilt of personally going against the Lord's express command to go forth and multiply by secretly going on the pill from then onwards.' So, the girl had at some time been sufficiently close to her mother to receive her confidences.

'He asked no questions. It's never been difficult to persuade him that everything in life that falls out fortuitously is according to the Almighty's benevolent command.'

Matt sighed. 'It doesn't stop him petitioning for grandchildren though, giving God a nudge with some heavy-handed hints to you and me.'

Grace tossed her head. 'He knows very well that I'm never going to be lumbered with brats of my own. I work all day most days with other people's. I thought you'd let me off the hook, though, and provide me with lots of nephews and nieces.'

Matt refilled his cup and drained it before speaking again. 'What would you say,' he asked Grace eventually, 'if I told you I already had?'

Without a pause, Grace asked, 'But Luke's hardly going to satisfy Father, is he?'

Each for his own reasons, Mitchell and Hanson sat rock-still and silent.

Grace laughed mirthlessly. 'Come on, Matt. I'm not stupid. Why else would an unsuitable, brassy blonde demand a private audience on degree day? Something that left you sheet-white and on automatic pilot for a week afterwards? Something that made you decide to get your feet under the company table straightaway when Father was prepared to pay for a post-graduate summer of traipsing round Europe?'

'Why have you never said anything?'

'Because you didn't. Besides, you had enough people telling you what to do. What happens now? Do we take Luke under our wing and blow the parents?'

Matt stared at her. 'How did you know his name?'

Mitchell had been silent for long enough. 'Yes, Miss Hanson, how did you?'

At various times in his progress from police constable to detective chief inspector, Browne had suffered undeserved strictures which he well knew were the result of a chain of resentment, passed down through the ranks and originating in an irritable outburst from one of the upper hierarchy. He determined, therefore, that none of his team should suffer because of his own indignation, still hot after a night's sleep, at Superintendent Petty's ironic congratulations on their progress with this case.

'Well done, Tom. That's the longest list of serious suspects I've seen in a decade. Might as well run a check on their wives, grandmothers and second cousins. With luck, there might be a trip abroad in it for someone.' Perhaps the super's youth had been back in the days when people spent their whole lives within walking distance of their

169

own small villages. Whatever the reason, he was always aroused to feeble sarcasm whenever an enquiry took even one of his officers further than Leeds or Bradford.

Browne anticipated a sober, somewhat pessimistic briefing, and looked back with regret to the not-so-distant ones when Hunter and Mitchell had sparred acrimoniously, whilst the recently departed Richard Dean had added fuel to their fire. It had often been exhausting but there had been little harm meant and a great many good ideas had come out of it. Above all, in those days there had been sufficient people to get the work done. None of the bright sparks who had been promoted out of his team to other parts of the West Yorkshire force had been replaced. Certainly, droves of extras were usually drafted in for a murder hunt, especially a double murder, but it was not the same.

Browne supposed it would have been worrying if his sergeant and his son-in-law had not matured enough to stop their constant bickering. It was time both of them moved on too. He understood Benny's lack of promotion. If he had not shelved his studies so that Browne's pregnant daughter could complete hers, he would have been the first to blame him.

He did not think that Hunter would ever move on now. The sergeant had been terrified when Benny had first transferred to CID that he would be overtaken in the race for promotion, but with that fear allayed, he now seemed quite content to continue writing his second unpublished crime novel, sing in his choir and now to produce another child, rather than seeking advancement.

As the three officers he had summoned quietly presented themselves and glumly regarded him, Browne could not be sure if they too were overwhelmed by the number of people who had wished Susannah Farrar to oblivion, or whether, in spite of his efforts to sound positive, his expression appeared to them aggrieved and bad tempered. He repeated Petty's comment, making a joke of it, then, seeing they were not amused, hurried on with the morning's business.

'I've got the report on both post mortems. Ledgard does little more than confirm the speculations we've already heard.'

'Anything on the Smiths' car rug?'

'Afraid not, Jerry. Apparently, young Vanessa stuck it in the washing machine whilst the stains were still damp, and it came out sparkling clean to the naked eye. SOCO managed to pick out where the blood had been but they couldn't isolate anything he could compare with the samples he's taken from the body.'

Jennie broke the short silence that followed. 'In a way, I see what the super means. No one's very sorry that she's dead, just the sister a bit for old times' sake and perhaps Wendy Allen for the same reason. The parents would have reacted more strongly if they were not both so ill, but no one's come forward, as a partner or as a friend, or even an employer, and said any more for her than that she had a good brain and could be amusing. Even her son seems quite happy without her.'

'Maybe the super's right with his suggestion, too,' Mitchell offered. 'If either of their wives had somehow found out that Milton or Singh was shelling out all that money . . .'

Browne groaned. 'Look, we're obviously having a watch kept on the four men, as far as manpower allows—'

' . . . and there's Grace Hanson,' Mitchell finished determinedly, ignoring his CI's interjection.

Hunter grinned. 'For good measure, why don't we add Shahnaz Singh's father? You know, to protect the family's dignity and keep the family money to be spent on his legitimate granddaughters.'

Browne looked startled. 'Have either of you any reason for thinking that any of these folk knew what was going on?'

They shook their heads, but Mitchell added, 'I don't

think I could shell out that sort of money every month without Ginny finding out.'

Hunter smiled, then asked, 'What did you mean about the Hanson woman?'

Mitchell briefly described his session the previous afternoon with the Hanson family. 'She's an obstetric physician. She was doing part of her training in a Bradford hospital when Luke was born there. She recognized Susannah, and Luke was the first breech presentation she had to deal with so she's remembered him ever since.

'Matt and Grace are twins. They seem very much in cahoots. At first, I was wondering if she might be providing an alibi for him, but now I'm beginning to wonder if she could have done it to get him off the hook and he's covering for her. They've only got each other's word for where they were after about nine forty and the parents live well on this side of York.'

Jennie frowned. 'If she's known all that time, why should she suddenly decide to take matters into her own hands now?' She considered this question for a few moments, then added, 'Perhaps we should ask that about all of them.'

'The new baby.' They all looked at Mitchell. 'I was thinking about the Singhs, I mean. They've just had yet another daughter in a culture that chiefly values sons, so Singh risks coming to Cloughton to inspect the one he thinks he has got, and discovers he hasn't.'

'Or,' Hunter added, catching Mitchell's enthusiasm, 'in frustration, when Shahnaz produces a fourth girl, Singh taunts her with it. Then she determines to get rid . . .' He shook his head. 'No, I'm getting fanciful.'

'Hanson and Milton only discovered quite recently that they'd both been defrauded,' Browne reminded them. When no more suggestions seemed to be forthcoming, he asked for Hunter's account of his visit to Kevin Wilson.

Hunter obliged, dwelling on his chance meeting with Lisa and her revelation of her father's late evening trip that he had failed to mention to the police. I didn't go back in to challenge him. I wanted to think about it first and check with his firm.'

'What did they say?'

'The chap who'd know wasn't there. He's seeing me at ten.'

'Can you fit in Craig Reynolds, Jane Griffin's boyfriend, after that? He's waiting in for us.'

As Hunter noted the address, Browne's telephone rang. He listened to it, smiling, said, 'Yes, send her up,' into the handpiece, and to his team, 'A breath of fresh air for us. Vanessa Smith is back.' After a few moments, Caroline Webster tapped on the door and brought the girl in.

Vanessa was unselfconscious and intent on the purpose of her visit, quite certain of her evidence this time and excited at her small part in the chase. She accepted Hunter's chair graciously, showing no embarrassment as he proceeded to pace the area of floor behind her. Jennie scribbled as the girl explained how her surveillance of the bus station had come about.

'In broad daylight this woman wasn't a lot like the dead girl, except for the hair and general build. What I recognized this morning was something about how she moved and the expression on her face. I'm prepared to swear in court this time.'

'That's good. Would you tell us absolutely everything you can remember about her.'

The girl nodded at Browne, making no coy disclaimers about the brief glimpse that she had had or about the distance between her and the woman. She closed her eyes to shut out distractions. 'She was wearing low-heeled court shoes, and thick, dark tights. She had a straightish skirt in a dark colour and a red anorak. She walked as if she was either tired or fed up, but quickly. She didn't have much time to get her bus. She nearly missed it.

'She was carrying a shopping bag in her left hand, big and patterned. Her hair was pulled back in a pony tail. It

173

looked silly. I'm not sure how old she is, but too old for that and it didn't go with her clothes.' She opened her eyes and returned Mitchell's grin.

'I bet you revise for exams by just calling to mind how the notes look on the page of your notebook.'

She looked startled. 'Yes. I can do that, actually.'

Browne brought her back to the point. 'I suppose you didn't notice which bus you saw her alight from?'

'I couldn't see the number but it was stopped in bay C five.'

'What time was it?'

'Between eight thirty-five and eight forty. I lost sight of her when she turned downhill on platform A, but then the 401 came up to the exit road and she was on it, still on the steps. She must have flagged the driver down after he'd started off and she was still waiting to pay her fare.'

Browne glanced at his watch. It was now ten minutes past nine. There was little point in getting the nearest patrol car to follow the bus. It might even be back in town if the 401 route was a short one. He smiled at Vanessa. 'That's very detailed and useful. Is there anything else?'

'It was her right sleeve that was torn on Saturday and her right arm that was bleeding.'

As Caroline was dispatched to return Vanessa to school, Mitchell was already thumbing through the local bus timetable he had grabbed from Browne's shelf. 'The 401 goes every twenty minutes between town and Old Mill Bank. There's a loop at the end, starting and ending at the Golden Sovereign, on Stebbing Lane, but most of the route's out and back on the main road.

'We'll have to ring the transport people for the other bus. The timetable book won't tell us what stops at bay C five.'

Browne had anticipated his comment and was already making enquiries. He grimaced at the information he was given but thanked his caller for it. 'It's the 311. Crossley Bridge, about three miles further out than the hall, is one furthest point. The other is Dean Royd at the far end of Canal Road. It's a figure of eight route with the bus station the crossing point in the middle. The bus that gets to bay five at the relevant time is from Crossley Bridge.'

Mitchell was already looking up the route. Browne went over to the large-scale map of Cloughton on the wall opposite the window and held out his hand for the book. Mitchell surrendered it, unwillingly.

'It seems reasonable,' Jennie suggested, 'to suppose she was on her way to work. What sort of places are there close to the 401 route?'

Browne was busily tracing with his finger. 'Not a lot that I can see. No factories or office blocks, anyway, but there are several pubs and shops and a restaurant.'

'Bit early to be selling anything. Perhaps she's a cleaner there.'

'I doubt it, Benny. She could get a cleaning job without having to travel so far, and she was wearing court shoes and a straight skirt.'

Jennie defended Mitchell's point. 'She'd want to look reasonably smart to travel. She had a shopping bag. She could have had her working gear in it.'

Browne shrugged and returned to his map. Having studied it for a further few moments, he went back to his desk where he busily filled in action sheets. 'Transport people for you, Benny. See the drivers of those two buses. They are all one-man jobs, aren't they? See if the woman travels regularly, where she got on and off, whether they know her.'

Mitchell did not resent these elementary instructions. He knew they were an indication of the CI's excitement. He tried to imagine what reason the woman might have for not coming to them of her own accord to report her assault on Saturday. She must know that whoever attacked her very likely killed Susannah. Why was she not offering them all the information she could, if only for her own protection? Why could she possibly want to protect her attacker?

Chapter Sixteen

Mitchell had to wait in the doorway of Cloughton Transport Department's canteen. The air inside was filled with steam and bacon fat. The two men who preceded him both wore spectacles and had been blinded on entry. Trapped behind them, he surveyed the bustling scene over their shoulders whilst they polished their lenses vigorously, one with a pristine white handkerchief and the other with the front tail of his grubby shirt that he had hauled with difficulty from the protesting waistband of his trousers. The huge room was noisy. More conversation was being shouted from table to table than was muttered between any of the men and women who sat together at them.

Mitchell looked along the service counter. It was not surprising that the majority of customers were overweight. There was little on offer that was not encased in pastry, and the biggest of the colourful placards behind the counter proclaimed the amazing value for the punters' hard-earned money of the establishment's all-day breakfast. It seemed to consist of every type of food that could possibly be fried and, judging by the illustration that accompanied the words, it was probably so named because it would take the average person all day to eat it. Mitchell had no mean appetite but he doubted whether, having consumed one, he could have hurried off to another shift of physical work.

As he looked round, the man he had come to see

rose and signalled to him. Mitchell offered him further sustenance by semaphore and, when the man nodded, joined the short queue to procure bacon butties and almost solid-looking tea.

Malc was thin, surly and unforthcoming except with complaints. He had driven the eight thirty-five bus on the 401 route and remembered the woman who had flagged him down just as he was pulling away. 'I'd have ignored her. Departure time's written plain enough in the book and on the sheets in the bays, but the fat cow on the front seat pointed her out to me and the whole load of them were shouting. When I let her on, the silly bitch hadn't the right money. It was early. I hadn't any change in the box.'

'Where did she sit?'

He shrugged. 'How should I know? I drive the bloody bus, not organize a dinner party on it.' Then, intimidated by Mitchell's best glare, 'She went inside, not upstairs. That's all I can tell you. A flaming inspector got on at the first stop by the town hall and was fussing round, poking into everything.'

'Where did she get off?'

Malc finished his tea and crammed in the last of his butty, as though fearing that Mitchell might withdraw what was left of his offering if deprived of information. 'I've no idea.' He chewed for a few more moments, then, in a slight effort to be more conciliatory, 'I suppose I'd have noticed if I'd had to stop specially for her, so it was probably somewhere where a whole crowd were put down. Could have been outside those flats by the football ground, or at those shops beside the Sovereign where the loop begins. What with her and all, I got back too late for a proper breakfast.'

Mitchell was unsympathetic. 'At least you didn't have to pay for it. Now, perhaps, you could point out Bert Hopper to me.'

The second interviewee proved to be the character who

had cleaned his spectacles on his shirt. Mitchell estimated between nineteen and twenty stones of him and wondered how he managed to tuck them all behind a wheel. The man had contrived his own variations on the drivers' uniform. The standard trousers and jacket were enlivened by a Fair Isle sweater, vigorously patterned but mercifully faded. His bedraggled tie, possibly rescued from the cat, was tied over a collar that had been intended by its factory machinist to fold casually back and was making every effort to do so.

Bert had queued while Mitchell talked to Malc and his tray was loaded with the raw materials for the maintenance of his fine figure. He frowned between forkfuls in an effort to produce some helpful facts.

'Customers are thin on the ground at the Crossley Bridge end of the route. Most of the folk living up there travel in swish cars that won't let the buses move out. My passengers are mostly their skivvies and do they have some tales to tell! I could pass on a few facts about those nobs that would brighten up the front page of the *Clarion* if they got out.

'There's quite a social life on that early trip as we all tell each other what we'd like to say to our bosses – me included. I couldn't give you many people's names, though. We just know each other's faces, and sometimes a first name, but we know each other's life histories, and what papers we read, and all about our children's schools or jobs.

'That little girl who got done in at the hall used to go up on the 311, though it was the trip after the one you're interested in.' Mitchell felt quite hopeful as he described their mystery woman to him. Bert's eyes indicated that he remembered her, but he had to wait until the current, gargantuan bite of egg and fried bread had been masticated and swallowed. 'She was a bonny lass,' he confided, wiping his mouth on a handkerchief. Glancing at it, Mitchell understood why it had been deemed unsuitable for

179

cleaning spectacles. 'She looked drained, though. I have seen her before, but she wasn't really a regular – sometimes there, some days not. She didn't join in the chaff, didn't say much at all. She got on two stops from the Crossley Bridge terminus. Agreed with me that it was a nice sharp morning, then she sank into the first available seat.'

Bert made another stop for refuelling, chewed, swallowed and continued. 'The others mostly sit further back. It's part of the fun to bellow down the length of the bus to me. I think she was deliberately avoiding getting involved, couldn't be bothered with us. Seemed to have a lot on her mind. When we got into the bus station she was the first to get off.

'She seemed in a hurry but I didn't watch her any further. I was swapping insults with the rest as they got off.' He glanced at his watch. 'Got a few minutes yet. I fancy another cuppa and I think a vanilla would nicely round that lot off.' He pushed back his empty plate and heaved himself to his feet. 'Want one?'

Mitchell restricted his request to more stewed tea. He watched Bert's huge bulk lumber across the room, reflecting that there, but for the grace of Ginny and his rugby trainer, went the future Mitchell.

Hunter was not best pleased with his lot. He was not resentful, but certainly disappointed. He considered Vanessa Smith's sighting of the injured woman their best break yet in this case, and Mitchell, as usual, was the one to follow it up. Yet he recognized that his trip to Bradford was a piece of his own unfinished business. He wanted to see it through and clear up any doubts about this man he had liked on sight.

Surely Wilson had enough trouble on his hands without becoming embroiled in secret midnight assignations, whether with his sister-in-law or anyone else. Besides, he had seemed to Hunter to be a genuinely contented family

180

man apart from the current difficulties that would have upset any household's smooth running. He was proud of his young daughter's maturity, patient with his mother-in-law's bizarre behaviour and obviously concerned for the strain it caused his wife.

He had made no secret of his dislike for Susannah. Hunter's imagination painted a scene in which the expressed dislike was a cloak for something very different, in which Wilson contemplated a change of partner and was turned down by her; in which, in the unlikely setting of a vandalized bus shelter, he'd had his revenge.

Hunter's instinct told him that that wouldn't do. He turned a corner and parked neatly in the forecourt of the Yorkshire Provident Building Society. The building was familiar to him but he had never had reason to go inside. The revolving door delivered him into a foyer like that of a three- or four-star hotel, restful, with a suggestion of luxury, but impersonal.

The security officer at the reception desk was unimpressed by Hunter's warrant card and gave him an escort rather than directions to Mr Roberts's room. The door read, tersely, 'Maintenance Manager'. The office into which it led, though not spartan, was more homely than the appointments below. Mr Roberts too looked homely. He gave Hunter his visitors' armchair and confirmed that Wilson had indeed been on call on Saturday night and that his services had been required to deal with a computer breakdown.

'And the call-out was at ten fifteen?'

He shook his head. 'I thought it was nearer midnight, but I'm afraid that, for once, the call was not properly logged. Immediately after I'd called Wilson in, I got a message from my wife telling me our daughter had gone into premature labour. I'm afraid the next half-hour was spent on domestic arrangements. But it can easily be checked out.'

Hunter nodded and raised a hand to avoid a long

181

explanation of how this would be done. 'Is Wilson a reliable worker?'

Roberts hesitated. 'He used to be and he certainly knows his stuff, but it can't be long now before we have to pension him off. Bad arthritis in his hands. Pity. Still, he'd soon be thinking of retirement in the normal way of things.' He stopped as he noted Hunter's puzzled expression. 'Just a minute. Are you asking me about Brian Wilson?'

'Kevin.'

'Ah!' Mr Roberts had obviously met this mistake before. 'Good friends but no relation. But you were so definite that it was last Saturday night you were interested in, so I didn't ask. Kevin's never on call on Saturdays because it's one of his wife's working nights. They sort it out between them, so long as one of them is available. Kevin covers on Tuesdays, Wednesdays and Fridays.'

Hunter felt disappointed rather than excited and, even in the face of ten years' experience as a detective sergeant, looked for a way out for a witness with whom he had felt such an affinity. 'If his colleague's hands were particularly bad, might Mr Brian Wilson have appealed to Kevin, especially if he thought his job was on the line?'

Roberts shook his head. 'Kevin's a soft touch. It's the sort of thing he might have done but he didn't this time. I'd dashed off to get a message to my son-in-law who works here in another department. Brian was just arriving as I came back through reception.'

Hunter gave insincere thanks for the information he had been given. He wondered if he could contrive another meeting with Kevin Wilson before he had to report back to Browne. First, though, he'd better attend to his second commission.

He ran Craig Reynolds to earth in one of the few houses in the row opposite Crossley Hall that was not privately

owned. Number twenty-four had been split into two flats
on the first and second floors and three large bed-sitting
rooms leading off the ground floor hall. It did not yet
show a lack of the care withheld by dwellers in property
that belonged to a landlord. Someone obviously still
cleaned the brasses, weeded the garden and washed the
large expanses of white paint.

Reynolds occupied a room at the back that overlooked
the garden and which had originally been the house's
dining room. A tiny breakfast room, little more than a
large cupboard, linked it with the kitchen, which he shared
with the occupants of the two larger front rooms. In the
main room Hunter saw a tea chest and two large cartons,
labelled, in felt-tipped capitals, respectively 'CROCKERY'
and 'BEDDING', the latter empty. They occasioned his first
question. 'How long have you lived here?'

'About a month.' Reynolds's allegiances seemed many
and various. His chest was pledged, in garish colours, to
Dire Straits. Working with Benny all this time had taught
Hunter that Dire Straits was a rock group, but he feared
it had not yet taught him to refrain from pigeonholing
rock enthusiasts together with the lower forms of life.
Reynolds's shoulder was dedicated, in the form of an
enamel badge, to Manchester United Football Club, and
his first waking thoughts, judging from the huge poster
on the wall facing the bed, to an alternative world peopled
with creatures half human, half werewolf.

Hunter gathered, from the conducted tour he had been
offered, that the untimely death of his girlfriend had not
left the young man too grief-stricken. Exclaiming joyfully
over his breakfast room, he had explained, in detail, how
having the water supply enter the house at his side of the
kitchen had enabled him to install his own shower there,
plus a hand basin.

'I still have to use the communal loo in the hall, but at
least I can wash, shave and so on without having to queue.
I shall have my cooker put in here too, when I can afford

183

one. For now, I'm afraid it's the primus, but I can produce quite good coffee.'

Hunter accepted the implied offer and demanded of Reynolds's unsuspecting back, 'where were you on Monday afternoon?'

He turned, his smile fading. 'Oh, yes, sorry. I was at Timeform, turf accountants on Winston Street.'

'Making a bet, or do you work there?'

Reynolds looked up from his crockery carton, a pottery mug in each hand. 'I didn't last Monday. I shall do next. I was being interviewed.'

'Successfully, it seems.' Hunter seated himself, uninvited, on the edge of the bed and watched the youth fill his cafetière with boiling water.

'Well, yes, but it's only a temporary appointment for a year. Still, it gives me time to look round, and it's easier to get work if you're in work.'

'The address, please.'

'Half a sec.' He scrabbled in a drawer and emerged triumphant with a piece of paper. 'This is the letter inviting me. The address and phone number are on it.' He handed it over, then went to fill the two mugs. Hunter took his and sipped from it as he read through the letter and folded it into his notebook. 'I'm really looking forward to it.'

Reynolds prattled on about his forthcoming duties until Hunter placed his empty cup beside the cafetière. 'I'm sorry to see you so upset about Jane Griffin. Just remember, time is a great healer.'

Reynolds looked offended. 'She wasn't the great love of my life, you know.'

'So I gather.'

'She messed me about a good deal. It was just that our parents were friends and ever since we were about fourteen or so we've gone out with each other whenever one of us was short of a partner for a particular occasion. There have been long gaps when we didn't see one another at all.'

'Quite. So you're saying that it hasn't hit you yet that she's really gone for good and when it does you'll be really upset.'

'Yeah, that's it.'

'Do you know anyone who might want to kill her?'

He shook his head. 'Well, no, not for her own sake, but I heard it was because she had some information to give the police about Saturday night.'

'Such as what?'

'How should I know? Anyway, that's what her mum said, for one, and that Wendy at the hall, and Clare thought she might know something. She always had her ears flapping.'

'Clare?'

Reynolds made himself comfortable in his only arm-chair. 'I'd better explain from the beginning.'

'What a good idea!'

He eyed Hunter warily. 'Yes, well, I said we only saw one another on and off. A few weeks ago we started knocking about together pretty regularly.' Hunter sighed. 'And then she cooled off again and started standing me up if she could find a date she liked better.'

'Annoying for you.'

'What? Oh well, she'd done it so often that I had a couple of flings myself to get my own back and the latest one I really fancied. For a while it didn't cause any problems.'

'No?'

'Not really. With being unemployed, I was always available. Jane worked days, Clare works nights, so I worked both shifts with whichever one was around and kipped when I could. It was nice while it lasted. I didn't want it to end like this though.'

'A sensitive person like you wouldn't.'

He smiled at Hunter uncertainly. 'When Jane didn't turn up on Monday night, I thought at first that she was sulking because she'd found out that I took Clare to the opening of the Blue Dahlia, that new nightclub down below the railway station. I'd asked Jane to come originally but she didn't know then that she'd have to be at the hall for that weird concert.'

'But you've just said Clare works nights.'

Reynolds sighed as though Hunter were a particularly obtuse child. 'That's right. She does the night shifts at an old people's home just up the road from here. She goes in at eight and it's all stations go for an hour and a half or so, getting them settled into bed. They're usually all down by half nine, unless there's an entertainment laid on and there wasn't last weekend. After that there's nothing much doing till seven next morning when they start getting them all up again.'

'So Clare goes walkabout in between . . . How does she get away with it?'

'The older woman she works with is very easy-going. If there's something special going on they'll cover for each other, once everyone's asleep. The other woman even went to sleep herself last Saturday. Clare had to wake her up when she got back in.'

'And the name of this convenient place of work?'

'Crossley Lodge.'

Chapter Seventeen

Coming off duty at six o'clock on Saturday morning, Caroline Webster decided that without a cup of coffee, even the canteen variety, she wouldn't make it back to her flat. Not that she hadn't found her completed shift fun. She supposed 'fun' didn't seem quite the word she should be applying to helping with a murder enquiry but, however the DCI might frown on such an attitude, she was finding herself highly entertained.

Of course, she still thought walking her normal beat a bit of an adventure. You met all sorts and the perks offered by the shopkeepers on her patch had considerably improved both her diet and her wardrobe. Better than her old job as a boring building society clerk any day. Better paid, too, though doubtless, before long, she would stop feeling rich and would join in with the general grumbling about police pay.

The queue at the counter had edged sufficiently far along for the sticky cakes under their glass counter to begin their seduction of her. She pulled her eyes away resolutely, grabbed a cup of black coffee and looked around for somewhere to sit.

There was a space beside lucky, skinny PC Michelle Jackson. Caroline tried to measure the therapeutic effect of her cheery conversation against the trauma of having to watch her consume her huge cream doughnut, then moved quickly, realizing that the seat was the only vacant one in sight.

'Going off?'

Michelle shook her head. 'No. On in a few minutes. I've to go up to Crossley Lodge. They've had a break-in.'

Caroline followed the progress of a blob of jammy cream from plate to mouth. 'What's worth pinching from an old people's home?'

Michelle licked her fingers daintily. 'Drugs cupboard bashed in, general damage, radios, TVs and money gone, even sweets.'

'How can they – from people that age?' Michelle, her mouth refilled, gestured her shared disgust. Suddenly, Caroline's sympathy for the deprived elderly was forgotten. 'Did you say Crossley Lodge?' She pushed aside the revolting, milkless coffee and stood up as PC Jackson wiped her mouth and consulted her watch. 'Can I come with you? Our case has a connection with that place.'

Wendy Allen was accustomed to lie in on Saturday mornings. The hall's opening at ten made her lying abed akin to many people's early rising. Nevertheless, she made sure that all her administration and paperwork was finished before the weekend and, the previous evening, she had told Luke that if he woke before eight fifteen he must amuse himself and not disturb her.

He was an obedient child but, by eight o'clock, she had realized that she had omitted the vital adverb 'quietly' from her warning. Still, she smiled to herself. He played very well and the music made a pleasant background to her drifting in and out of full consciousness. Until last Saturday, she had never thought of the recorder as anything but a child's toy. She realized, wryly, that quite a few of her current conceptions were new, since last weekend.

When the alarm rang at a quarter past the hour, she got out of bed, showered and dressed in a black sweater and skirt. Never before had she worn these two garments together to form such a funereal outfit. She had never accepted that big people should creep around apologetically in dark and dowdy colours, and then, yesterday morning, Luke had looked her up and down as she came to breakfast in a brilliant emerald dress.

He had made no comment and she had thought at first that he was upset at her insensitivity in parading such a cheerful colour within days of his mother's death. Then, as he buttered the one piece of toast his mother had allowed him each morning and watched her consume her third, he had volunteered, casually, that his mother had had a black dress to wear when she thought she needed to lose a few pounds. Wendy had felt ridiculously wounded.

She refused to capitulate and remove the dress, but she was sufficiently anxious for his approval to half-cover it with a dark woollen jacket that had only added to her girth and made her sweat. The boy had something in common with his mother after all. He made everyone anxious to please him.

As they sat at today's breakfast, they heard the letter box snap, followed by the soft thud of packets hitting the mat. Luke waited for her nod that gave him permission to fetch them. Of the four letters he brought in, she consigned two, unsolicited – from a local travel agent and a national charity respectively – unopened, to the wastebin.

The next was addressed to her in an unknown hand, and the one below, in that same hand, was for Luke. She glanced, too late, at the postmarks of the two letters. Otherwise, she would have kept back the child's until she had read her own. She told herself that her motive would have been to prevent Luke suffering any further trauma but, as he washed down his toast with milky coffee, he did not appear in the least upset.

The truth was that she was jealous of the child's liking for Adam. She pushed the thought away and concentrated on the boy. It worried her that, throughout the week, at least as far as she knew, he had not shed a tear, nor shown

189

any other sign of distress. His manner had been subdued but it had amounted to very little more than the restrained good behaviour his mother had always demanded.

Wendy's own letter announced Adam Holroyd's intended arrival in Cloughton that night. He would stay in the hotel she had recommended last weekend, having found it very satisfactory. He expressed his gratitude to her for her care of his son. ' . . . I feel guilty for not having relieved you of responsibility for him already, but I can see that you, too, are fond of Luke and will understand that I want to get to know him gradually and introduce the great changes he must face as and when he is ready for them.' She gripped the closely written sheet so that her knuckles whitened. ' . . . If by any chance he is not still with you, I would be obliged if you could pass Luke's letter on to him.'

Wendy tried to analyse her fury. She was not the maternal type or she would have produced a child of her own, though without the unwelcome encumbrance of a husband. That was easy enough these days. But it was just this child she wanted, handsome, sensitive, with an adult seriousness that seemed strange in the offspring of Susannah – maybe he was Adam's after all. Though, when she thought about it, living with Zannah would force any child to become self-reliant.

Luke gave her a delighted smile. 'He's coming back. Mr Holroyd, I mean.'

As she gave him permission to leave the table, Wendy wondered if she could whisk the boy away for the rest of the weekend, prevent the meeting. No. It was inevitable. The man's determination to have his way came through to her, partly from his firm and flowing handwriting. The boy's was evident as he returned to the dining room carrying his recorder and the sheet of music Adam had given him.

Shahnaz Singh tucked tiny Amrita back in her cot and settled three-year-old Manju to threading wooden beads

190

on to a brightly coloured bootlace before she went back into Urfan's little study. She had opened the desk drawer earlier that morning just to borrow his paper knife and there the tickets had been. There they still were, with the details she had remembered – date: the following day; destination: Faisalabad for two adults and three children. For airline officials, babies like Amrita did not exist. No mistake.

Shahnaz sank on to the edge of Urfan's office chair. He wouldn't do this to her. She shook her head, rested her chin in her cupped hands and remembered her father, whom she had equally trusted, showing her an envelope of innocent French airline tickets. Remembered too the policemen who had called only days ago and her husband's refusal to explain their business.

For the first time, she felt angry with him. Not for the tickets, whatever the explanation for them proved to be, but for trapping her at the hinge of two cultures. She had been brought up an English schoolgirl. Her skin was brown but she had fitted in here, and the few aspects of her home life that made her different her teachers and friends had found interesting.

Her unlooked-for trip to Pakistan and her meeting with Urfan had made her aware of her Asian heritage. Before that it had consisted of half-listened-to stories of her father's that never impinged on the reality of school prize-givings, friends' birthday parties, English shops marking out the English year with their January sales, Easter eggs, summer beach clothes and Christmas trees. She had loved her holiday in the Punjab and the strange, quaint village life. It had been a temporary game she had played, a background that was part of Urfan's charm for her, but not what she could endure as inescapable daily conditions.

And Urfan had shown only thankfulness for the sophistication and physical comfort of life in England. He had come a long way, in every sense, from the village where he had been his father's fourth son. There had been a family business of sorts that had failed to flourish because its profits were drained by the maintenance of four families. It would not support a fifth. A marriage had had to be arranged for Urfan with a distant cousin. He had been an embarrassment his father had been glad to be rid of, but her father-in-law had done his fourth son a bigger favour than he knew. Now Urfan could buy him out many times over.

Could that be his plan? Her mind recoiled in horror. But why the hurry? And why the secrecy? Could it be that the tickets were not intended for her family? Shahnaz stood up and began to pace the rooms of her beloved house, smiling as she watched her third daughter's absorption in her self-appointed task. Urfan's manner had been a little odd for a couple of weeks now. Even before the policemen came, she had had the impression that, for some reason, he feared that the privileges her father had lavished on him might possibly be withdrawn.

But, even if Urfan had, in some unlikely way, offended her father, he had nothing to fear. Urfan was in charge of the business these days. If he pulled out of it now, her father would be the loser.

Suddenly she came to a decision. If she was making trouble for Urfan, then it would be his fault for not confiding in her. She would consult Inspector Blay. She picked up the receiver of the telephone on the desk and punched the buttons rapidly before she could change her mind.

Hunter's hope of giving Kevin Wilson another opportunity to explain his movements of the previous Saturday night were frustrated by his chief inspector. Browne came into the station foyer behind him and ushered him up the stairs to his office as he described his session with Wilson's employers. 'Let's have him in now and put the frighteners on.' Hunter looked alarmed until Browne elaborated, 'I'll find two tight-lipped PCs to escort him in silence.'

'What about Mrs Farrar?'

Browne considered. 'Julie Wilson will probably be at home on a Saturday morning. She'll just have to stay up and hold the fort till her husband gets back. It should give him all the more reason to give us what we want from him as quickly as possible. The young daughter might be around too, but we'll make one of the PCs a woman just in case.' He grabbed his telephone receiver and gave instructions. 'When he gets here we'll stick him in an interview room for long enough to work up a sweat. Oh, to have Richard back for ten minutes to give him the inimitable treatment.'

'Do you think Wilson's our customer?'

'For the moment let's just say he's got a lot of explaining to do.'

Browne picked up a scribbled report from his desk and glanced through it. 'It looks as though Benny's been and gone. Let's see what we can make of this.' He took the report on Mitchell's efforts with the two bus drivers over to the wall map and drew a circle with his finger, its centre the relevant bus stop and its radius half the distance between the stops on either side. 'Our mystery woman got on the 311 two stops after it left the terminus. If she was on the way to the sort of work we envisaged this doesn't seem the right kind of area for her to live. We've got two farmhouses and their surrounding fields, about twenty rather grand houses with large gardens, and Crossley Lodge, that very superior home for the elderly where the Wilson woman works.'

'What about the other end?'

Browne drew two more imaginary circles round the places where the driver of the 401 had suggested his mystery passenger might have alighted. 'Here we've got small houses and a huge block of flats, and further on a row of shops and a pub. We'd better see if she worked in any of those. The red anorak and the pony tail should be a good enough description.'

A tap on the door announced Mitchell, breathless and

193

apologetic. 'Sorry to be late. I nipped along to ask Malc the Misery how much fare the woman paid. He remembered because he hadn't enough change for her. It was fifty-five pence so she'd have ridden further than the flats. The pub and shops would be about right.'

'The Wilsons live in the parallel street above,' Hunter said.

There was an electrified silence, broken by the two younger officers speaking together.

'Wilson said his wife's bad arm was troubling her.'

'The boy said he'd helped mind his grandmother whilst his aunt saw the doctor.'

There was a further silence of a different quality as they pondered the significance of Julie Wilson being the woman they sought.

'So are we to assume that Kevin Wilson left his mother-in-law and children asleep and went out to attack his sister-in-law and wife?'

'But why should he?'

'Maybe Julie was hurt whilst trying to protect her sister.'

'But how would she know anything about it? She was at Crossley Lodge.'

Browne answered all these questions with the same comment. 'We'd better ask him. But, first, we'd better give young Vanessa a sight of Julie Wilson to confirm that we're right. It certainly makes sense if she was going not *to* but *from* work. We'll have to get Julie here as well and she'll probably take a lot of cracking. If she's protected her husband so far, she won't just cave in now.'

He grabbed the telephone again. 'Has that car left for the Wilsons' yet?' A quacking of excuses came over the line. 'Well, hold it. I want two cars and at least two WPCs. Kevin is to be picked up first, then, when his car's out of sight, the other one picks up his wife. Don't be heavy-handed with her. You'd better leave a couple of our women to cope with the children and the old lady.'

On his second circuit of the office for that session,

Hunter paused. 'We could do with finding the pub he rang them from. Whatever he told them, it must have seemed imperative. Susannah left her young son on his own at a concert and Julie left all her old folk completely unsupervised since she'd turned a blind eye to her assistant going gallivanting at that new nightclub.' He resumed his pacing, then stopped again. 'I don't suppose they had a live pianist there.'

The telephone rang. As Browne listened to his caller, his eyebrows disappeared into his hair, and when he put the receiver down after a couple of minutes it was with a gusty sigh. 'Just when we thought we were narrowing the case down to something manageable! That was Inspector Blay from Leicester. It looks as though Singh's about to do a runner.' He gave the gist of Blay's message.

'Perhaps it's on legitimate business,' Hunter suggested, without much conviction.

Mitchell, more practical, asked, 'Have we got enough on him to try to stop him?'

'We've certainly got the right to know where he is. Gough's in Leicester, tailing him. I'll warn him, get him to check in to me a bit oftener, then we'll play it by ear. Who wants to entertain Mr Wilson?'

Hunter shook his head. 'I don't. I like the bloke. He seems an ordinary, well-meaning husband and father, doing his best for his family in hellish circumstances.'

'And he's snapped?'

'I suppose so.'

Mitchell shook his head and scowled. 'I don't see how it could help him to attack the two sisters. It's the mother-in-law who's causing all the problems.'

'When you boil over you act instinctively,' Browne reasoned. 'He doesn't seem to have been over-fond of Susannah.'

'He called her a cow when he was talking to me. Wouldn't he have pretended to like her if he'd ...? No, I suppose someone would have told us they didn't get on and then it would have looked worse for him.' Hunter subsided.

'Why is Singh skipping off to Pakiland?' Mitchell demanded from his perch on the windowsill.

Browne frowned at him. 'We can do without the aggro that sort of terminology causes.'

Mitchell was unabashed. 'But, does he think we're on to him?'

Browne sighed. 'Not necessarily. He could just be afraid of his father-in-law. When the papers get on to this case, they'll have a real birthday, and Asians get pretty worked up when they think one of their number has disgraced them, especially if a white girl's involved. There was something in the *Clarion* last week about an Indian in Bradford who shot—'

'Who's being racist now?'

Hunter hurriedly distracted them. 'Singh's alibi for Monday is shaky. He spent most of it alone doing paperwork or driving around seeing people, one of them as near as Huddersfield. Not that I can see him doing Jane any harm. How could he have known she had anything to tell us?'

'We don't know that Singh, or Hanson for that matter, wasn't up here. Only that Milton was.' Browne decided the discussion was going nowhere. 'Jerry, can you organize a more detailed check on Singh and Hanson for Monday? Benny, you take Wilson, but let him stew for a while first. I'll see if I can get Jennie in to try the effect of tea and sympathy on Julie.' Anticipating Mitchell's question, he added, 'I'm going to put my feet up whilst I wait for one of you lot to come up with the goods.'

Chapter Eighteen

When Kevin Wilson had waited twenty-five minutes in interview room three, Mitchell opened the door quietly and looked in. Wilson was sitting, half sullen, half forlorn, his hands on his knees. He stared fixedly at an area of floor that was relieved only by a crumpled chocolate wrapper and one highly polished shoe containing the right foot of PC Martin, who sat opposite him.

Mitchell dismissed Martin with a nod and stood aside to let him pass through the doorway. Taking the vacated chair, he made himself comfortable but still did not speak. Wilson raised his eyes.

Seeing the appeal in them, Mitchell abandoned the abrasive questions he had planned, asking instead, 'Want to get it off your chest?'

'I want to talk to my wife.'

Mitchell laughed. 'I expect you do. You'll need to prime her with the story you're going to tell me. It's a pity, for you at least, that you didn't take that precaution with Mr Roberts. Sergeant Hunter had a chat with him yesterday, which left us rather disinclined to believe all that you're going to tell us now. So, I'm asking you again, do you want to get it off your chest?' Wilson nodded. 'Like some tea?' In response to a second nod, Mitchell rose and made the request to Martin who was outside the door.

Wilson's voice was a monotone. 'I don't know where to start.'

'Begin with the pub where you made your phone calls.'

Wilson looked up again. 'Pub? What phone calls?'

Mitchell's sympathy was short-lived. 'I can't help you if you're going to play dumb. Start wherever you like.'

Wilson's gaze returned to the floor. At the crown of his bent head, Mitchell could see the beginnings of a bald area. Wilson had the sort of fine hair that never seemed to last much beyond early middle age. Maybe that was why the man kept it so short, or maybe he was aiming at a hard appearance to mask his soft nature. Mitchell fingered his own almost equally short but thickly sprouting thatch with satisfaction.

Without raising his head, Wilson began his account. 'It started with Julie letting Clare Kennedy go out with her boyfriend, last Saturday night when they were both supposed to be on duty. She pretended she didn't mind but, actually, Julie always agrees because she can't refuse people, can't assert herself and say no. That's why she got landed with Ma. Maybe it's even why she married me.'

Having embarked on his story, Wilson seemed to relax slightly and looked up again. 'Anyway, once she was on her own, one of the old ladies became ill. She had chest pains and Julie knew it was serious as soon as she answered her bell. She was a bit frightened and rang for an ambulance. The old woman was frightened too. She clung to Julie and wanted her to go with her in the ambulance. The ambulanceman wanted her to as well, to calm the patient down. Getting so upset was making her worse.

'Julie daren't admit that Clare wasn't in. There should always be two people on call but ringing for assistance would have meant that Clare was sure to be missed. Julie just locked the door behind her and went to the hospital.'

'That was very foolish of her.'

'Yes, she realized that afterwards.'

There was a tap on the door. Mitchell opened it and accepted the tea tray, hoping the interruption would not stem the flow of Wilson's tale. Thankfully, he realized the man was anxious to go on. He accepted his cup with just

198

a nod of thanks. 'As soon as the old girl was safely settled in a ward, Julie said she had to get back and then realized that the buses at that time of night were only going up to Crossley Bridge on the hour. She was frantic to get up there quickly so she found the visitors' phone on the bottom corridor and rang me.

'I was down there with a coat over my pyjamas in five minutes and had her back in a quarter of an hour. She asked me not to tell anyone so I said nothing, even to Lisa – except that when she woke up and asked, I had to tell her the story about having to go to work.'

He had become hoarse and stopped to drink deeply. Mitchell gestured an invitation to refill his cup and, seeming glad to have his hands busy, he attended to Mitchell's too as he went on speaking. 'On Sunday morning, after we'd heard about Sue, I wondered if we ought to tell the truth, rather than mislead the police, but we soon decided to leave it. We had nothing to do with the murder and didn't want to get mixed up in it, and if the home manager heard what had really happened, Julie would be sacked.

'She was so scared, she actually got round to telling Clare that, in future, if she's supposed to be at work, she stays there.'

He fidgeted and fiddled with his cup, waiting for Mitchell's reaction. Mitchell got up and took a turn, Hunter-fashion, round the tiny room whilst Wilson kicked at his chair leg. Successful murderer he might or might not be; a comfortable liar he certainly was not.

Mitchell settled himself again but made no comment on the story he had just heard, merely asking, 'How did your wife hurt her arm?'

Wilson looked more at ease as he replied. Maybe lying got easier with practice. 'That happened earlier on Saturday evening. One of the old ladies that Julie was bathing suddenly accused her of laughing at her, mocking her skinny body. She went for Julie and smashed a bottle of bath oil and Julie got a nasty gash before she could calm her down. It should have been properly cleaned and two or three stitches put in, but again, she couldn't ring for help or Clare would have been missed. She just drew the edges of it together with sticking plaster.'

'Why didn't she get it treated while she was at the hospital?'

'She daren't wait. She'd locked the old people in and was terrified there would be a fire or something. They smoke in bed if they aren't watched . . .'

Mitchell's tone suddenly changed. 'Wilson, stop wasting my time with all this crap. We know and you know none of it happened like that.'

Wilson leapt up, His chair overturned behind him. The table in front of him rocked and delivered its load of empty cups, pot and tray on to Mitchell's lap. The door flew open and Martin shot in. Together he and Mitchell escorted a sobbing Wilson back to the cells.

Jennie Taylor's interview with Julie Wilson was proving equally frustrating. Both the tea and the sympathy that Browne had instructed her to offer had been summarily rejected and Julie remained passively uncooperative. 'There's nothing I can help you with, but if I can't convince you of that, at least question me at home.'

Jennie considered that a hospital bed was where her interviewee ought to be. Her face was deeply scored by lines of worry and weariness and she held her arm awkwardly, obviously in pain. The voice, though, was strong and angry. 'I've got three young children and a demented mother who's afraid of strangers. You've left two young girls with them and neither looks much older than my Lisa.'

Jennie sighed. 'They're capable and experienced, but if you want to relieve them you only have to tell me the truth about what happened on Saturday night and you can go. We did try to question you both at home. You must admit you weren't very helpful.'

When there was no response, Jennie went on in a more hectoring tone. 'You're not doing your husband any good telling lies for him. You have a duty to your sister as well, you know.' She watched the woman blink back tears and relented. 'At least change your mind about some tea. Have you had any breakfast?'

Julie shook her head. 'Just tea, thank you. Look, you aren't asking sensible questions. If you think my Kev harmed anyone, even somebody he disliked as much as Sue, you must be mad.'

'Who hurt your arm?'

'Not Kevin.'

'Who then?'

The answer came in an insolent monotone, due more, Jennie thought, to an effort to keep control than a wish to offend. 'I was bathing Mrs Hunt. We think she might have been assaulted when she was a girl. Anyway, for some reason, every so often she turns on one of the staff, never another old person and never a man, and accuses us of laughing at her or intending to attack her. Then she goes for us. Usually her attack is feeble and easy to deal with. You just have to soothe her, make a fuss of her. Unfortunately, the bath oil bottle got broken and in her excitement she picked it up and I was cut.'

'But she wasn't? In her excitement, she picked up a piece of broken bottle, sliced up your arm and didn't even nick her finger?'

'Would you have been pleased if she'd needed stitches?'

'No, just more ready to believe your story.'

The tea arrived. The young PC doing sentinel duty brought it to the table and, having poured it, Jennie watched in silence until the woman had drunk it and put her empty cup down on its saucer. They rattled together until Julie managed to disentagle her trembling fingers from the cup's handle. Then, at a nod from Jennie, the door was opened once more, this time to admit Vanessa Smith.

*

201

At noon, Browne called his team together briefly to collate their experiences and to map out the next half day of the investigation. There was a general air of despair since none of them thought the morning's efforts had achieved anything.

Jennie described Julie Wilson's defence of her husband's story, even in the face of her meeting with Vanessa, her would-be rescuer. 'The girl did just as she was asked, sympathized about the arm injury, then asked why she'd run off from the hospital. Julie never batted an eyelid, said her arm was doing nicely, which it obviously isn't, and stared blankly at the question. Then she said she must have a double.'

'What did the girl say?'

Jennie shook her head. 'It threw her a bit. I thought for an awful moment that she was going to recant, but after they'd taken Julie down, she said she'd only been stuck for a reply that wasn't ill-mannered. She's definitely prepared to testify that it was Julie she drove to the infirmary on Saturday.'

'Right, Benny?'

Browne nodded to Mitchell who described his unproductive interview with Wilson. 'Funny thing is,' he added, scowling ferociously at no one in particular, 'I somehow felt that, apart from the story he admitted to, about being called in to work, he was telling the truth.'

Browne's telephone rang. When he swore into it, the attention of his team was riveted on him. Although he bore strong language from some of his team quite phlegmatically, he almost never used it himself. He was apologizing already. 'That wasn't meant for you, Gough. I just haven't enough men to keep a twenty-four-hour watch. I'm coming over. Meanwhile, watch the old man.'

'The Singhs have skipped?'

Browne answered Mitchell with a curt nod. 'Any suggestions?'

Mitchell, as always, had one. 'We all need a bloody

good lunch.' He nodded at his father-in-law. 'Especially you.'

It was the ambition of all the poor people in Cloughton to live in Crossley Bridge and of most of the rich people in Crossley Bridge to buy up and live in Crossley Lodge. Caroline Webster climbed out of PC Michelle Jackson's car, parked in front of it and surveyed it. 'You can't tell that it isn't just a gracious old family house,' she offered, impressed.

PC Jackson sniffed and activated her central locking system. 'It's probably in the by-laws that whoever owns it isn't allowed to alter it.'

Carol nodded as Michelle followed her up the steps. 'It's a pity that the folk here don't appreciate more than the comfort of the chairs and beds and the number of TV sets they've got.'

'That they had till last night, you mean.'

As they were admitted, Caroline began to feel she had been unjust. Michelle went into conference with Mrs Gray, the home's manager, who had already made as efficient a list of missing goods as was possible when their rightful owners were in their eighties and nineties and rather unreliable even on the subject of their own possessions. Certainly, her list of missing communal property was complete. Michelle asked questions about the items and no one thought it strange that Caroline elected to mix with the old folk.

Many of the old people were very positively occupied. Several were reading, one or two engrossed in books rather than just leafing idly through magazines. Caroline remembered passing several cases full in the hall. A game of cards of some kind was being played at a table in the bay window, and at a smaller one by the fire, two old men frowned seriously over a chess problem. Another man strummed at the huge old upright piano against the longest wall, ropes of veins standing out on the backs of his hands. Caroline knew from the hollow, ringing tone that the instrument had an old-fashioned iron frame. As she stood behind the man, he glanced round at her and began to sing the tune he was picking out.

'Knee deep . . . in flowers we'll stray,
We'll keep . . . the showers away,
So, if I kiss you, in the garden,
In the moonlight, will you pardon – me.'

The old man eyed Caroline lecherously over his shoulder. Several of the other inmates had joined the chorus, rusty, quavering voices, painting in the notes with streaky brush strokes. Caroline found Mrs Gray standing beside her.

'Until recently Mr Lydgate used to earn himself pocket money playing in the local pub,' she said proprietorially.

'How recently?'

She shrugged. 'Oh, he gave up three or four months ago, but their loss is our gain, isn't it, Bert?' She put her hand on his shoulder.

'They all seem very busy,' Caroline offered.

The woman nodded. 'It's our policy. They all do as much as they can, wash up and so on. Some of them even do a bit of the cooking if they're fit enough not to be a danger to themselves. It's much quicker if we do every-thing ourselves. In fact, we could manage with a couple less members of staff, but they're happier this way. You can see the benefits.'

Caroline nodded. 'A friend of my mum's works here,' she remarked, mendaciously. 'Mrs Wilson.'

Mrs Gray beamed. 'Lovely woman, very good with them, but she only does four nights. She's off at the moment, anyway. She's hurt her arm and she's got family trouble. Well, you'll know about the Farrar murder. Mrs Wilson's her sister.'

Caroline sat beside Mrs Gray on a blissfully comfort-able sofa and lowered her voice. 'I suppose the old folk find death very depressing, frightening even. It must remind them that their own isn't far off.'

Mrs Gray shook her head. 'Surprisingly not. "We've had a death" is announced to their visitors with as much excitement and anticipation of a break in routine as you'd expect for a wedding or a christening. They seem inured to the thought of their own demise and love helping to arrange the funeral.'

'That old lady isn't joining in the fun.' Caroline indicated a woman who sat a little apart, a magazine disregarded on her knees.

Mrs Gray nodded. 'Her friend died just over a week ago. They did everything together. She's missing her but she'll come round in a few days. As a matter of fact, Mrs Wilson is anxious to have the vacant room for her own mother. She didn't like the idea of putting her away but she has Alzheimer's and things are getting pretty impossible at home. Here would be a good compromise. The atmosphere's good and she'd be able to put her to bed herself several nights a week.'

'She'll be coming, then?'

Mrs Gray gestured her frustration. 'We'll have to see. Her sister was going to help financially. Our fees are more than the government would allow her even if she qualifies for a state grant. What happens now will depend, I suppose, on how Miss Farrar's money's been left. I don't want to put pressure on Julie just now, but I shall need to know one way or the other fairly soon.'

Caroline stood up suddenly and tapped the pianist on the shoulder. 'Can you play "Lily of Laguna"?'

There were loud and universal groans. 'Did you 'ave to?' asked the woman who had languidly toyed with the magazine, suddenly perking up. ''E plays it twenty-four hours a day. We'd only just got 'im off of it and on to "Tiptoe"!'

The pianist put a creaky but still competent arm round Caroline's waist and poked at her left breast with stiff

205

fingers. His right hand strummed and his rheumy left eye winked at her.

> 'I . . . know she likes me,
> I know she likes me, because she says so . . .'

The old voice cracked only on the sustained notes.

> 'She is my lillee . . . of Laguna,
> She is my lillee . . . and my ro-o-se.'

Jennie Taylor sidled guiltily into the canteen, feeling very little interest in the killing of either Susannah Farrar or Jane Griffin, except to feel sorry for them. She was a part-timer on the case and on every occasion she reported in for duty, some further information had given a new twist to the investigation. She could make no significant contribution because she was spending so much of her time on duty catching up with what had occurred whilst she was off.

And, when she was off duty, she spent more time quarrelling with Paul and mentally apologizing to Lucy than she did in enjoying being at home. Before Lucy was born, she would never have sneaked in here, would never have wanted to, for an unscheduled break when she should have been sifting through files, absorbing information. She queued for coffee, then turned to see Mitchell devouring a sausage sandwich with an enjoyment quite unspoiled by guilt.

She sat opposite him and remarked acidly, 'We'd neither of us be here if the CI were in his office.'

Mitchell lifted the lid of his second sandwich and anointed the sausage with tomato sauce before looking up at her. 'True.'

Jennie's spirits dropped still further. 'Don't tell me you're in a black depression too. That would be the last straw.'

206

Mitchell looked strangely ill at ease but shook his head. 'No, I'm quite happy. I'm just working my way round to saying something.' She refused to help him and he continued, haltingly. 'About four years ago, I was two-timing Ginny, having a fling with that special, Joss Wade, who was killed at a concert.' She nodded, remembering. 'In only about a couple of dozen words, you gave me the roasting of my life about it. I've never forgotten.'

She stared at him, astonished. 'Don't tell me you've been grinding your axe all this time.'

He grinned. 'No. Every word was both true and necessary. I've been waiting to return the favour. Now you need someone to roast you.' He bit into the sandwich again and chewed in silence.

Eventually she asked, 'What about?'

Mitchell pushed his plate away and plunged in. 'Jennie, stop taking it out on the rest of us because you can't give the work one hundred per cent any more. Just go at it full tilt when you're here and remember that sooner or later you'll be back full time. And drop all this defensive women's lib talk. You used to be amused when the CI wanted the woman's angle, thought it put you one up on us all, and pretty often it did . . .'

He stopped speaking as Jennie drew a white envelope out of her pocket. 'I hear what you're saying, Benny, but I've made up my mind the other way. I'm resigning. I was keeping this back until the case was cracked but you've just decided it for me finally. I'm going to hand it in today.'

Mitchell stood up abruptly and took a step away. 'I should have kept my big mouth shut.'

She smiled and pulled him down again. 'It's nothing to do with you. I'm pregnant again. I think, subconsciously, I let it happen to make sure there was no going back.'

Mitchell grinned at her. 'This isn't the Cloughton nick, it's a bloody baby factory. Have a sandwich to keep your strength up.'

She accepted and waited for him to bring it. She hoped he would continue to sit with her whilst she ate it and he did, though his head was down and he looked at the table rather than her. 'So, you're going too – and Richard and Nigel and Robin have gone already. It's the end of an era for me in this nick. And the flat I was so proud of seems claustrophobic now, there's certainly no room there for another infant. It looks like it's decision time for all of us, Jen. I shall get my head down after this case, apply for all the study leave they'll give me, pass my sergeant's exams and then apply for every post that comes up wherever it is. Ginny's welcome to begin her MA, but she can fit it around the kids and she can find a course wherever I find a job.'

Jennie judged that his resolution to change his life with no recourse to Ginny's wishes would probably not outlast the morning. They were laughing together, at themselves and at each other, when Caroline Webster burst in excitedly. 'Sergeant Bennett told me the CI and Sergeant Hunter have gone to Leicester and that you were in here.'

'So, now you've found us. What's all the excitement about?'

'Would you buy the notion that the phone call that got Susannah Farrar out of Crossley Hall came from her sister?' Caroline embarked on an account of her visit to Crossley Lodge and Bert's lecherous serenading of her. ' . . . and so that's where the piano background to the phone call came from. What if Julie got Susannah out of the concert to argue with her and—'

'But why?'

'Because Mrs Gray, in charge of Crossley Lodge, told her she had to decide quickly about taking the vacancy there for her mother. Suppose Susannah met her and—'

'And what?'

'I don't know much about her. Maybe they argued about money, began fighting even.'

'Fighting in a Gucci suit!'

208

Mitchell grinned. 'She might wear them now – or until last Saturday anyway – but she wasn't born into them. Once a street kid, always a street kid at heart. You're talking to one.'

'So what now?'

Mitchell shrugged. 'Well, it's a first, anyway. We've never before sent the old man off on a wild goose chase and had the case all wrapped up for when he came back. Only...'

'Yes?'

'Which of us is going to tell the super?'

Superintendent Petty required confirmatory evidence from Kevin Wilson before he was prepared formally to arrest his wife on any charge whatsoever. This time, interview room one was chosen. The table stood two inches higher than the one in room three. The chairs were of dull orange plastic rather than wood-grained vinyl. There was no chocolate wrapper on the floor but, instead, two squashed cigarette packets in the region of the wastebin testified to the bad aim of the previous occupants. The windows here were marginally cleaner. None of it made any difference to Kevin Wilson.

Mitchell's voice was sympathetic and the sympathy was genuine. 'We've got it all sorted now, Kevin. You can stop worrying. You've done your best for your wife. Now we'll do our best for your whole family.'

Wilson looked up warily and blinked. 'When can I see her?'

'I'm not sure. My boss has gone haring off to Leicester after someone else, but I'll arrange it if I possibly can. She's in good hands. We've got our doctor to re-dress her arm. When you've just answered a few more questions, we'll take you home to your children and see what can be done about your mother-in-law.'

'What questions?'

'For a while, you really believed that tale you were

209

telling me just now, didn't you? The one that Julie told you last Saturday night. When did you realize what had really happened?'

His relief at being able to tell the truth was palpable. 'Not till she'd had the nightmare on Monday, after she'd killed that little girl. I heard her yelling and screaming and went up. She'd told me about it before she'd roused up enough to know what she was saying. It's a hell of a mess and I don't know what to do about it. What I do know is that Julie wouldn't have been able to keep it secret and live with herself, even if you hadn't found it out.'

'Start at the beginning then.'

Wilson fixed his eyes on the wall behind Mitchell. 'She wanted Ma in that nursing home of hers so that she'd have contact with her but not the responsibility. She asked Sue several times if she'd help with the money but that selfish cow said they were a one-parent family and the money might not always be coming in as it was doing now.'

'So, what did Julie want to discuss so urgently on Saturday night?'

'Julie was exhausted. I think she just flipped. She got Sue out of the concert by saying Peter was much worse. She waited outside Crossley Lodge to be picked up, then she went for Sue, verbally, I mean. Sue just repeated calmly what she'd said in the afternoon, said there was no point in further discussion and she'd take Julie back. They were just about at the bus stop where Sue was found. She started to make a three-point turn.

'Julie screamed that she wouldn't have anything more to do with her. She wouldn't even accept a lift back. She jumped out of the car whilst it was still moving and staggered to the bus shelter. Sue thought she'd hurt herself, parked the car and came to see.' Wilson's voice was bitter. 'Couldn't have Julie in the wars or she might have been landed with the old girl herself. They struggled there

210

and Sue was hurt badly, accidentally, I think.'

'You think?'

He said, dully, 'I don't know what was in Julie's mind. She had a pair of tights ready in her pocket. When I picked her up at the hospital, she pulled them out in mistake for her handkerchief.' He pulled out his own and blew his nose hard. 'Julie hurt her arm on some of the glass in the struggle. She was frightened. She hadn't really faced up to what she'd only half planned. She was in a daze when that little girl, Vanessa, stopped to help her. What will happen to her now?

'She was driven to it, you know. I don't condemn her for what she did to Sue. I wish I'd saved her by doing it myself – but I can't live with what she did to poor Jane Griffin.'

For the second time that day, Wilson was escorted, weeping, from an interview room. This time, though, it was to a waiting car and home.

Epilogue

Adam and Luke were spending the morning packing up Luke's belongings, ready for his final move to Bath. Outside, the late spring made the neglected garden beautiful. There was still much new ground to break in their relationship, so that neither of them had found the task tedious. Nevertheless, by eleven o'clock a rest was indicated by aching arms and backs.

Luke took his can of Coke into the garden. Adam perused the current edition of the Cloughton *Clarion* as he sat on the bottom stair to drink coffee from the thermos flask he had brought with him. Running his eye down the 'hatches and matches' column, he noticed two items of mild interest.

HUNTER To Annette and Jerry, a welcome son (Christopher William), a long-awaited brother for Timothy and Felicity. Mother and baby doing well.

The Hunters, Adam reflected, seemed to like long names. The other contribution was briefer.

MITCHELL To Virginia and Benedict, a daughter (Caitlin Mairead).

Adam wondered what West Yorkshire teachers would make of the Irish names in four or five years' time. And Declan was a soft sort of name for the strapping nearly-

212

three-year-old he had seen on the force's rugby field with Mitchell yesterday morning. The boy was already showing a fair turn of speed, with a ball tucked under his arm, repelling the attacks of its rightful owner, another officer's child. He liked the Mitchells and was grateful for the hospitality he had been offered in their smart new house as struggled to sort out his rather complicated family affairs.

He turned back to the front page, where a long involved account followed the banner headline, CLOUGHTON WOMAN GIVEN PROBATION FOR INVOLUNTARY MANSLAUGHTER OF SISTER. So, Browne had achieved his aim of getting the two killings tried separately. He wondered how much good that would do Julie.

Adam was glad to see the article mentioned Luke only once and gave no indication of where the boy would make his future home. Nor was there any reference to Susannah's blackmail of her seducers that had made her seemingly so rich, though, in fact, the chief assets she had bequeathed to their son were money from insurances and the house. The lawyers had been willing to make some money available for Luke's education, but Adam was becoming ever more convinced that it would do the boy good to experience the rough and tumble of the local comprehensive when his senior school had to be chosen this coming year.

He grimaced as he swallowed the lukewarm dregs in the bottom of the plastic cup, before taking out the letter which Karen had sent on to him from Bath. He re-read it slowly. Was there any point in agreeing to the 'get-together for old times' sake' that Matt proposed? Adam suspected that Matt had been put up to writing the letter. Either Singh or Milton probably hoped to put moral pressure on him to make them some financial restitution out of Susannah's estate.

He owed them nothing, though he felt some sympathy. Any attempt at compensation ran the risk of Luke discovering his mother's duplicity and none of her victims was destitute. Milton's wife was successfully representing her Birmingham constituency. Matt, apparently, confessed all to his parents and had been forgiven, and Urfan had been offered a total amnesty by Shahnaz's father on condition that he brought the grandchildren back to Leicester.

Adam consigned the letter to the plastic sack of rubbish. Luke came in from the garden and stowed his empty can tidily away in the same black plastic sack. Together they returned to his room.

'What a lot of things you've got.' Adam indicated a pile of boxes, already tightly packed. 'You'll need a furniture van all of your own.'

The boy turned to him. 'I didn't always want the things I was given.'

'Did you sometimes want things you weren't given?' Adam felt absurdly pleased when the boy nodded. 'Is there something I can give you to celebrate our getting to know each other at last?'

Luke frowned, considering the request. 'Could I have one of those metal stands to hold my music?'

Adam was amused. 'I wouldn't need to buy one. There are dozens at my house.'

'Well, perhaps I could have a flute, if they're not too expensive.'

'You'd like to play the flute?' The boy's expression answered him. 'Fine, you can begin quite soon, in a couple of weeks or so. I can show you the basics myself whilst I'm looking around for a good teacher. You really ought to play the piano too.'

Luke was prepared to be obliging. 'That's all right. I'll do both, if we can afford it.'

'I don't think that's going to be a problem. Your mother paid lots of insurance contributions in case anything happened to her and you were left on your own.'

'But I'm not on my own, am I? I've got you and Karen. Tell me again what your house is like.'

214

'It's quite big, perhaps even bigger than this one, but it's in a row, joined to the houses on each side.'

'You mean terraced.'

'Yes. It's Georgian. Lots of houses in Bath are. It's got lots of rows of oblong windows but it isn't smart like this one. I've been sending quite a lot of my spare money to your mother to help look after you and I spent all the rest on instruments and music.'

'That's all right. We'll carry on doing that.' Adam smiled at the boy, amazed how little like his mother's his values were, how little she had contaminated him. 'I don't understand why she told me you were dead.'

'Neither do I, son. Neither do I.'

'I'm glad you're not. Can I have my room right at the top, in the attic?'

Adam laughed. 'You can have all four of them if you like, but I can only afford to put a carpet in one. Now, do you want absolutely everything here, or can we throw some things away?'

Grudgingly, Luke allowed his father to consign some battered board games and some nursery books to the plastic sack. Then, from the back of the wardrobe, he produced a small attaché case.

'What's in there?'

Luke flipped it open. 'Just some cards full of stickers. I collected them last year.'

'They're very colourful.'

'They came out of packets of Wheaty Whirls.'

'However many packets did you eat to collect all these?'

'Not many. My friends gave me all theirs.'

'Didn't they want to collect for themselves?'

The boy shrugged. 'They can't have done, can they? Anyway, I'm tired of them now. It was collecting them that was interesting. When I get to Bath, maybe I'll collect something else. Hold the sack for me while I stuff them in.'

215